Night Warriors
Beasts, Book 1

Brenna
Lyons

Veriel's Tales I: Crossbearer Turned

FIREBORN
PUBLISHING

Fireborn Publishing Copyright

Statement

Veriel's Tales I: Crossbearer Turned
Copyright © 2004/2005/2009/2015 by Brenna Lyons
Print ISBN: 978-1-943528-16-5
First Fireborn Publication: October 2015

Cover Artist: Brenna Lyons
Photo Credit: 123rf
Editor: Kathryn Lively
Logo copyright © 2014 by Fireborn Publishing and Allison Cassatta
Licensed material is being used for illustrative purposes only. Any person depicted in the licensed material is a model.

All characters and events in this book are fictitious. Any resemblance to actual persons, living or dead, is strictly coincidental.

This book is written in US English.

PUBLISHER

FIREBORN
PUBLISHING

PO Box 5216
Haverhill, MA 01835

Dedicated to...

My brothers and sisters, for teaching me that there is more than one side to any story.

John Malkovich's performance of Jekyll and Hyde in *Mary Rielly*, for confirming my belief that a man can be both villain and hero, driven to madness and torn to be what he can never be in either state.

Hollie...I *told* you Jörg was coming back!

My inability to believe that *anyone* can be all bad—or all good, even the Warriors.

Glossary of Warrior Terms

Beast- Beasts are what humans erroneously refer to as vampires. The stories humans tell are obviously not correct, but you can't expect a human to get everything right.

Blutjagd- The "blood hunt." Warriors crave battle with the beasts, as the beasts crave blood. Warriors are tied to beasts in that they sense many of the beasts' special powers. A Warrior can feel the use of coercion, feeding, and other controls of humans. They also feel other Warriors engaged in *Blutjagd*, the death of beasts and Warriors in their range, and the presence of nearby beasts that are not fully ghosted. Rigorous battle training will quell the *Blutjagd* for short periods of time.

Elder- One of the original beasts, the Stone stealers who were damned for their crimes against the Stone and the Warriors. The elders are gifted with powers turned beasts are not, including the ability to reproduce with a *Blutjagdfrau*, the ability to turn other beasts, and the inability to be killed by anyone but a Warrior.

Endspiel- The point in printing when a Warrior must either seal printing or go insane. A Warrior who feels printing may not progress should break printing long before this point. Note that they are rarely smart enough to do so.

Fluch- The Warrior's curse, passed from father to son or daughter. The *Fluch* may be removed from a daughter but never a son. If the *Fluch* is not removed in the *Zeremonie der Freiheit* by the time the menses begin or the *Zeremonie des Schutzes* is performed before freeing, the daughter is cursed to become *Blutjagdfrau*, a female Warrior. Because elders target *Blutjagdfrau* as mates, Warrior fathers will go to any lengths to free a daughter not marked by the Stone.

Ghosting- A talent that both beasts and Cursed Warriors learn to harness. Ghosting can hide the physical form of Cursed Warriors or beasts and all they hold or carry from each other and humans. In a lesser strength, it can "blur" the image of the user so that humans do not note the passage in particular but still see a person there, which avoids accidental collisions. Even a ghosted beast cannot hide uses of power that a Warrior can track. Warriors sometimes ghost in tandem to remain visible to each other but not other Warriors or beasts.

Krankheit- The "sealing sickness." In the final stage of the transformation between human and Cursed Warrior, at or about the sixteenth birthday in males and a year after the start of menses in females, the sickness strikes. The young Warrior will suffer nausea, vomiting, a high fever, disorientation, dizziness and may become incoherent. It is usually the only time in a Warrior's life that he or she becomes ill, save morning sickness in a *Blutjagdfrau*.

Printing- Like imprinting, a Warrior becomes tied to his mate for life. He cannot choose another if she's lost, cannot be unfaithful while she lives, and cannot ever divorce or otherwise dissolve the union. A printed Warrior is the most stable of men, unless his mate or children are endangered or lost. Then he will suffer the printing madness and may have to be killed by his house. Likewise, a Warrior who breaks printing, even early printing, will suffer for it. A Warrior who breaks printing too close to *Endspiel* will face the madness.

Veriel- The Mad Elder. The Destroyer of Lives. The Mad Deceiver, who led the traitors and freed the elders from the Stone. The most hated and hunted of all the beasts. Fixated on one woman, he would destroy the world to own her. Or... At least, that's what the stories say of him.

Warriors- Also called Cursed Warriors, *Krieger der Nacht*, *Soldat der Nacht*, or Sons of the Stone. The Warriors were an ancient race of protectors who spawned the beasts and now are driven to hunt their former brothers to extinction.

Crossbearer Turned

Kreuzträger Gedreht

The major players of the houses of the first cursed...

House Schwertträger (Swordbearer, later known as Armen)—
Gawen Lord Schwertträger, Stone lord, and his chosen mate Bavin
Regana, the chosen of Pauwel Lord Kreuzträger
Abbo and Marcwi, parents of Gawen and Regana

House Kreuzträger (Crossbearer, later known as Cross)—
Pauwel Lord Kreuzträger and his chosen mate Regana
Kethe, the chosen of Thorald, village leader
Andris, son of Pauwel and Regana and his chosen mate Berna

House Jäger (Hunter)—
Ditrich Lord Jäger and his chosen mate Anabilia

House Schmied (Smith)—
Cunczel Lord Schmied and his chosen mate Lela
Sibold of Schmied, master trainer to the first cursed and Stone lord

House Landwirt (Farmer)—
Gerhardus (known as Ger) Lord Landwirt and his chosen mate Ingela
Berna, daughter of Ger and Ingela and chosen of Andris Lord Crossbearer

House Maher—

Wilhelmus (known as Wil) Lord Maher and his chosen mate Evfemia
Riberta of Maher

House Kaufmann—
Olbrecht Lord Kaufmann and his chosen mate Lenne

The beast elders—
Jörg, the beast Veriel
Tilbrand, the beast Resten
Dado, the beast Lorian
Bertolf, the beast Draden
Redulf, the beast Carstol
Geldric, the beast Cerran

Major players in the village—
Eberhard, the leader at the births of the first cursed and elders
Marclef, the leader at the fall of the elders
Thorald, the leader after Marclef
Emecin, midwife and mother of Landric, the healer

Prologue

484 AD

Gawen marched over the uneven ground. The trees were thick but thinning as he neared the planting fields and home. His kill was slung over his shoulder. It was only a small deer, hardly larger than a wolf, but it would feed his family well. He hefted it as if it weighed not a thing. At nine, he was already the size of many of the smaller men in the village, and the deer was not a burden to him at all.

In a land full of tall, broad men with eyes as fair as a summer sky and hair the color of grain and fire and clouds, he was one of the marked. The Stone-Chosen were all dark haired—black except for the brown of Jörg's—and had deep brown or black eyes—except for the silver-gray of Jörg's and Wil's dark blue ones. Larger even than the largest of the local men in adulthood, the Stone-Chosen were giants even amongst the giants.

He scowled at the birthmark on his wrist. The blood mark given him by the Stone was the mark of *Syth*, the mark of the chosen master trainer and Stone lord. He was to be Sibold's replacement when the time came.

Most days, being chosen was simply what Gawen was. He no longer strutted about as if it made him important as he had when he was five and he had been given the duty of watching out for his younger brothers when they were brought to Sibold to play at battle with wooden weapons and hear the stories of the ancients that would define their places as protectors to the village.

Their formal training would not begin for many years—at fifteen. Gawen would be fully trained by the time the next, that insolent pup Tilbrand, was ready to begin his training. He secretly hoped Sibold would take on Tilbrand personally and knock the cocky attitude out of him quickly while Gawen worked with Wil. He would be a man of twenty-four by the time Jörg began his training.

Gawen knew Sibold and Eberhard, the village leader, were still searching for more of his brothers. The thought chilled him. They already numbered thirteen, and at times, controlling them was like reasoning with wolf pups.

He sighed at the thought that Ditrich would join the play in half a year.

Jörg was still a babe and would not join them for almost three years. When he did, it would be up to Gawen to shield him. Though Jörg had the blood mark of *Reg*—the intensity of the base of the fire, as proof of his status, prominent on the front of his shoulder, his features were different enough to cause dissention. With his rich brown hair and silver eyes, the difference had been noted immediately. Tilbrand had already been censured for wondering aloud if the difference in appearance denoted a weakness in the boy.

Sibold had high hopes for Jörg. He'd confided in Gawen that the Stone had named their youngest brother the greatest Warrior, their champion. Though Gawen was slated to lead, he would not be the strongest. He smiled at the thought that Jörg would be hard pressed to prove his place with twelve older brothers wrestling to knock him from his perch.

Strangely enough, Pauwel stood out as the shining star with his blood mark of *Ori*—the sun, even at only four years of age. If anyone would be a challenge to Jörg, it would be Pauwel, and Gawen was not sure that Jörg could live up to that challenge.

He furrowed his brow in concern. Being the most powerful Warrior made Jörg the weakest in other areas. He would be most unable to control his *Blutjagd*, most affected by printing, and most susceptible to being lost to madness. But, it was still a matter of many years before they had to worry about any of that. Still, the fact that Jörg's family's lands bordered his own was lucky. Sibold had given Gawen the duty of protecting their tiny, fatherless treasure as much as the fates permitted.

Gawen waved to a man from the village that was working cutting firewood; he sighed as the man bowed his head respectfully, fearfully. It had been millennia since more than two or three had been chosen by the Stone at once and more than a century since there had been more than one. The villagers were panicked and suspicious to have so many chosen.

Gawen hated the fear in their eyes. Even if there was a war coming, and by all reports it seemed there was, it was not the fault of the Warriors. Their duty was to fight to their deaths to protect all within the village. They were not the most pressing threat.

The *foederati* was unsettled. The peace was tenuous at best. It had been ten years since Sidonius had been exiled after his battle with Elric of the Goths.

Childric had continued the expansion of his father, Merovech of Chlogio, Chief of the Salian Franks, alternately allying himself with Rome and pushing the borders back to the Somme River. Three years in power, Childric's son, a man named Clovis, was attempting to continue the process of subduing friends and foes alike. His borders stretched out from the Pyrenees to the Rhine. Now, word was in the wind that Clovis and Ragnachar, his kinsman, would seek to take Syagrius at Soissons soon.

All these things were told him by Sibold, most of it knowledge imparted to the master trainer by the Stone. Gawen learned it all faithfully, knowing that the fight would eventually come to their village. Until then, it was a mass of politics and battles that had little bearing on this place hidden away from such things.

Gawen's people no longer bothered much with distinctions. In this region, only the tribe was of importance, only the village. Romans, Gauls, Christians, or Barbarians were of no importance here. Even the fact that Pauwel, the grandson of a Christian emissary who intermarried and produced an heir that now served the Stone of his grandmother's gods was hardly reason to wonder in a place like this.

Buried deep in mountains rich in iron and fertile for farming, the village prospered under the protection of the Stone. The Stone chose its people well, and the bargain had been sealed in blood and power. Every generation, a boy was born of a different family, chosen by the Stone to be its lord and confidant. On occasion, two were born...or three, based on the Stone's perception of the coming need of the village.

The Stone lord was always apparent by the mark of *Syth*. There were twenty symbols in the ancient language, and the Stone marked its choice of any of the aspects on its chosen—except *Zel*, signifying an end, *Jee* for Justice, or *Ani*—the sign of the birth mother of beast killers. Those were signs of war and death coming.

Tilbrand had been born with the sign of *Wul*—the cunning and feared wolf. It was a rare symbol, but it seemed appropriate for Tilbrand. Wilhelmus, Wil, carried the sign of *Len*—the strength of the mountain, and he was already a mountain of a young Warrior. Olbrecht had been born as *Baroo*—thunder, and Dado was *Pol*—the strength and speed of the horse. Cunczel was *Vin*—the untamable wind, Bertolf was *Nul*—the darkest night and stealth personified, and Redulf was *Iol*—immovable ice. Ditrich was *Dobler*—the twin peace bringer and diplomat, while Geldric was *Fih*—war personified and *Dobler's* opposite number. Gerhardus, Ger, was *Hir*—the cool depth of the wood.

For millennia, the Stone had protected the village, but many felt the coming situation was hopeless. Only once before in recorded history had there been so many chosen. Gawen knew that the villagers weren't sure whether to fear another beast war or an enemy so dire as to require thirteen Warriors more.

Sibold's magic should be sufficient to prevent beasts, but with the political situation, Gawen wasn't sure even the entire seventeen allowed blood marks would suffice. In the end, *Zel* and *Jee* might be required, and the village might be lost. In that case, Gawen would take the Stone away as was his duty, followed by whatever brothers remained, to find a new home.

Gawen speeded his step as his home came into view. For some reason, he was suddenly glad to be there. He wanted to run his hands over the baby growing inside his mother Marcwi, a brother or sister in blood that he had almost given up hope of ever having.

His breath caught, and he ranged his gaze over the group of people in the main room, his hand tightening on the edge of the rough door. His father, Abbo, wouldn't meet his eyes. Eberhard and Sibold stared at Gawen in a calculated way that made him uneasy, and he retraced his steps over the past few days to assure himself that he could not be in danger of censure for some misdeed.

When his gaze fell on Emecin, the young midwife who assisted Adalind as she learned her craft, peeking around Sibold's shoulder and looking grim, his blood ran cold. There was a problem with the baby, he guessed. His hopes of being a true brother seemed to crumble within him as he recognized the sound of weeping from his mother's bedchamber. The fates could not be so cruel! It was the only thing Gawen wished for, and they could not take it from him this way after all the months of hoping and watching the baby grow in Marcwi's belly.

Sibold smiled warmly. "Do not be concerned, Gawen. Come meet your sister." He turned and scooped a baby from Emecin's hands to show her to her brother.

Gawen smiled widely and dropped his kill on the table as he made his way to her.

She met his eyes evenly and seemed to assess him before yawning. She was newly born, still covered in a slick of their mother's blood and a milky substance he had seen on other new babies. Her eyes widened, as he stroked her cheek and hair with one huge finger. Her eyes were as dark as the night sky beneath a sea of black hair that was soft as down.

"She looks like me, Father," he exclaimed excitedly.

Abbo winced, then cast a sad look at his son, but Gawen gave it hardly a thought. Surely, it was an aberration of some sort. The Stone didn't choose female Warriors.

"Yes," his father agreed quietly. "Yes, she does, Gawen."

Sibold nodded his head. "You are her personal protector, Gawen. No matter what happens, it is your duty to keep her always safe."

Gawen furrowed his brow. "Of course. She is mine, a woman of my house," he replied seriously. A Warrior's duty to his house, especially women of his house, was taught early, before any other consideration.

"More than that, Gawen. The Stone demands this duty of you. Love and protect her as the Stone demands—with your life, if necessary."

He nodded soberly, unable to conceive of a duty greater than that to any woman of his house but accepting that it must be so if Sibold said it was. He put out his hands to accept her into his care, and Sibold placed his sister in his arms gingerly. Gawen laughed in glee, as she grasped his finger while he tickled her cheek.

"What would you name her, Gawen?" Sibold asked quietly.

Gawen looked at him in shock and dismay. "My mother?"

"She lives, though she is very weak. The child is yours, Gawen. What would you name her?"

He looked to his father, but Abbo shook his head and left, seemingly saddened. The door closed behind him with a chilling finality. Gawen felt his heart begin to pound. They really meant to give him this child as his own responsibility. They meant for Gawen to raise her as if she were his own. "Gana," he decided.

"Regana," Sibold corrected him. "Her name is Regana. The Stone approves of her name."

Gawen nodded quietly. "Regana." He smiled as she brushed her mouth over his fingertip, rooting for food, his concerns momentarily forgotten. "You hear that, little one? You are mine. You have to obey me," he ordered her.

"I never said that," Sibold interrupted him. "In fact, I wouldn't expect it of her."

* * * *

492 AD

"Tilbrand, hold," Gawen thundered. He bolted across the open area in the training building, his younger cursed brothers scattering in his wake. Gawen hit Tilbrand with a straight-arm to the chest, sending him crashing to the ground while he swept the troublesome, curly-headed child between them onto his shoulder.

Jörg took one look at Gawen's scowl and turned from the encounter, running for the safety of the group by the wall.

Gawen nodded at his retreating back. He tightened his grip on Regana as she tried to kick her way down. "Stop it," he grumbled at her.

Tilbrand found his feet again.

"Disarm," he ordered the unruly boy.

Tilbrand glared at him, but he sheathed his weapon. "I only wanted to teach them a lesson, Gawen," he fumed. "You let her run wild. She shouldn't even be here."

"You shouldn't be antagonizing the little ones," he countered. "If you left them to themselves," he smiled a crooked smile, "they wouldn't be forced to prove who is better trained. At least they understand teamwork."

Tilbrand darkened in anger. "This is the Warriors' training area, not a play area for little girls who need leading strings," he shot back. "You should have Eberhard's daughter nurse for you."

Regana fought her brother's grip, trying to exact her own retaliation for that remark.

Gawen crushed her to his shoulder with one huge hand. "Regana is my responsibility, no one else's. She will stay here under my care."

"Yes, she will," Sibold assured them, calmly walking to them, a disapproving look etched on his ancient face.

Gawen sighed as Regana stilled, then shrank closer to him. At least she had the common sense to be afraid of the master trainer.

He raised an eyebrow at Gawen. "Take Regana outside to wait for me," he instructed.

"Yes, Sibold." Gawen ground his teeth at Tilbrand's smirk; but from the indulgent look Sibold tossed after the tiny girl, he guessed whose side the master trainer would ultimately take—as usual.

In the tree line, he set Regana on her bottom. "Stay there," Gawen ordered as he sat beside her.

She raised her chin a notch, but she sat fairly still, a miracle in the making! Gawen took in the dirty face, red cheek, and the mussed hair critically before sighing and retying the thong that held her hair back. Regana fidgeted and shot him an annoyed look that warned of her intent to flee such ministrations, but she let him smooth her hair.

She looked to the doors of the training area nervously. "Is Tilbrand in trouble?"

"I don't know," Gawen admitted.

"He should be," she decided angrily.

"So should you," he reminded her.

"For what?" she demanded. "He struck Jörg for no reason."

"And you struck him."

Her face darkened. "Only in defense," she protested weakly.

"It is not your place to discipline the trainees. It is mine. All you did was anger Tilbrand. That's why he struck you."

Regana nodded, her fidgeting more pronounced.

"Now Jörg may be censured as well. He struck Tilbrand in defense of you." *And downed the older boy easily! Tilbrand—at fifteen and half again as tall as Jörg was—never saw the punch that knocked him flat.*

Her eyes widened, and she looked at him fearfully. "Jörg won't really get in trouble, will he?"

Gawen sighed. "I don't know. That is Sibold's choice."

Regana nodded miserably and curled under his arm for comfort. Gawen pulled her into his lap. At barely eight years old, she was less than half his height and tiny, even for a girl. But her stature hid more strength than Tilbrand had bargained for.

Gawen smiled, wrapping her in his arms and smoothing her hair. Regana had always delighted him, unless she was frustrating him or scaring him to death. He had never seen a little girl like her before. Gawen sobered slightly in realization; that was at least partly his own fault.

Abbo seemed to have abdicated all parental responsibilities the day Regana was born. When he'd walked out the door, he'd never come back as a father for either of his children. Marcwi had lived long enough to nurse and waste-train her daughter, but she was never the same animated woman Gawen remembered. She'd died when Regana was too young to remember her. For all that he was alive, Abbo had been as much a stranger to his daughter when he died shortly after his son reached sixteen.

That had left Regana almost exclusively in her brother's care. As much as Gawen enjoyed caring for Regana, he wondered if he was doing right by her. She had no females to learn womanly arts and attitudes from, and some of the things she picked up from the young Warriors were wholly inappropriate. Already, he'd had to correct some of the more colorful phrases she had been introduced to. Regana was learning to fight by watching the boys and by earning her lumps when her brother's back was turned.

Her closest friend and confidant was Jörg. His father had died before he was born, and his mother had been at a loss for raising such a spirited and headstrong child. She'd leapt at the chance to have Gawen guide him, as Sibold requested, and Jörg had attached himself to both Gawen and Regana immediately. The two were inseparable. From the first time they'd met, any trouble one had stumbled or run headlong into, the other had been involved somehow.

Gawen had worried about them playing in the woods between the houses, but he'd soon learned that nothing in the wood would dare hurt them. Whether they were blessed or simply too spry to be caught aside, he was surprised he hadn't gone gray prematurely dealing with them. Neither of them seemed to have any concept of the dangers around them.

Sibold smiled as he strolled toward them. Gawen wondered how he, Sibold's Stone-Chosen replacement and a military leader, had somehow become a nursemaid to all the children, but he supposed being responsible for them in battle and when they were walking the edges of madness had to start somewhere.

"You were always good with her," the master trainer complimented him.

"If only she would listen," Gawen noted in exasperation.

"You do not follow orders well, young lady," Sibold scolded her, studiously hiding a smile.

Regana looked at him shyly, then buried her face in Gawen's chest. Her brother sighed. Regana had always treated Sibold this way, despite the fact that it was obvious to everyone that the master trainer was akin to a faithful servant to her every whim.

"I don't understand it. She fears you for no good reason," Gawen complained.

"She doesn't fear me. She is fearless," the old man replied in admiration. "Regana?"

She peeked at Sibold, and he smiled.

"Did Tilbrand hurt you?" he asked.

She shook her head.

Sibold touched her bruised cheek gently. "You must become a lady soon, you know."

Regana scrunched up her nose in distaste. "I don't want to be a lady," she informed him stubbornly.

Sibold laughed. "What would you like to be?"

"A Warrior," she decided.

"That I cannot grant, though you might make a better one than some of those boys," he teased.

Regana smiled in response.

"No, you must learn to be a lady. Look on it as doing battle."

"I thought you wanted her to stay here?" Gawen asked in confusion.

"I do. Kethe and Evfemia could come here to instruct her. I'm sure you can impart household arts."

Gawen darkened. "I can, but I'm not sure she will learn it."

"She will if I tell her to," Sibold stated with a warning note that Gawen rarely heard where Regana was concerned.

The girl nodded solemnly, knowing that no one balked that tone with Sibold.

"See? She will behave for the older girls."

"I will believe it when I see it," Gawen muttered.

"She will, and someday she will wed a Warrior," Sibold imparted fondly.

Regana made a sour face at the idea. "Is Jörg in trouble?" she asked, changing the subject.

Sibold sighed. "I put him to work to keep him out of trouble, just as I am doing for you."

"But, it was Tilbrand's fault," she challenged.

Sibold smiled at Gawen. "I told you she didn't fear me." He met her eyes sadly. "Jörg must learn control, Regana. I know he believes he was only defending you, but he must learn to control his urge to fight before it controls him."

"What about Tilbrand?" she demanded.

"He has a special duty," he assured her.

Gawen arched an eyebrow at the old man. "He does?"

"I decided that Tilbrand has no appreciation for the sacred duty of those he must protect. Striking a defenseless child, a girl—"

"Defenseless?" Gawen laughed harshly at the thought of it.

"He pulled his blade, Gawen," Sibold reminded him.

He sobered instantly. "Yes, he did," he whispered, pulling Regana firmly to his broad chest.

"He won't do it again. I have stripped him of his weapons until the next new moon."

"That's more than two weeks away."

"You're right. For that period of time, he will be responsible for our two youngest children."

"Ditrich and Jörg will keep him busy," Gawen decided.

Sibold shook his head. "No. I meant Jörg and Regana."

Regana sank further into his chest. "We don't like Tilbrand," she pleaded with Gawen quietly.

His breathing seemed strangled. Regana was his responsibility, no one else's. "I don't like this, Sibold."

"He will not hurt them. I guarantee it."

"If he does, he will answer to me," Gawen promised.

"Only after I've finished with him."

* * * *

Regana sighed and dropped her sewing into the basket at her feet. She leaned on the wall and watched Gawen training with Wil.

"What is wrong?" Kethe asked, her blue eyes darkening with concern.

"I hate sewing," Regana moaned.

"You hate everything," Evfemia remarked.

"Not everything. Just everything a lady is supposed to do," she countered, kicking her feet at the long skirts in annoyance. The skirts were another of Sibold's ideas for turning her into a lady. Her face was washed, her hair neatly bound, and Regana hated every minute of it. She sighed once again. "I'll never be a lady."

"You won't be if you don't try," Evfemia noted.

"Doesn't a lady do anything interesting?"

"Like what?" Kethe inquired.

"Never mind. I'm going home. If I don't move, I'll go mad." Regana rose and started away, collecting the hated sewing.

Tilbrand met her at the doorway, looking forbidding. "Where are you going?" he demanded.

"Home. I can find my way," she assured him.

"No, you don't. I'm responsible for both of you. You stay or you both go."

"Fine," she answered from between clenched teeth. Regana turned on her heel and stormed to Jörg. "Come on," she told him.

"I have to—"

"I'll help you tomorrow," she cut him off cleanly.

"Sibold won't allow it," he protested.

"Tilbrand won't let me leave unless you do, too. Walk home with me and come back once he leaves. Please, Jörg."

Regana knew the moment she won. His scowl turned into a crooked smile, and he snuck a glance at Gawen before grabbing her hand and pulling her to the door a little faster than her skirts allowed comfortably. They tripped out past Tilbrand, Regana giggling at the end of Jörg's arm and gripping her basket of sewing. She loathed sewing and wished she could throw it off the highest peak.

"Come on," Jörg ordered Tilbrand in good-natured amusement. "We'll take up as little of your time as we can."

Tilbrand grunted his agreement and started walking, the two of them at his heels. Regana fought her skirts most of the way. It seemed she was constantly tripping over them or getting tangled in the hem. Several times, Tilbrand turned to give her dirty looks.

Finally, she retaliated. "If you want me to handle my skirts, carry the basket," she demanded of him.

"Have Jörg do it."

"In case you haven't noticed, he is keeping me from falling and hurting myself. You can do one or the other."

Jörg met her eyes in surprise.

"Give me the basket," Tilbrand barked.

Regana raised an eyebrow at Jörg as she handed the basket to the older boy. "Told you," she assured him.

"Come on," Tilbrand demanded. "If I have to play nurse, at least I can do it inside."

Regana looked at him in shock. "You're not staying," she decided. "Just see me home. I'll be fine there."

"That's not what Sibold ordered."

Regana shot a seething look at his back and started hiking her skirts into her belt in annoyance. Jörg looked at her in dismay, and she motioned him for silence. She cut her path in a diagonal and shot silently onto a footpath through the trees. Regana knew Jörg would follow her, so she didn't waste time looking to see that he did.

They didn't make a sound, when Tilbrand realized they were gone. They didn't slow their escape, when he roared out an order for them to return. He had no chance of ever finding them now, and Regana was determined not to let anyone order her life like this.

When they reached the great Oak, Jörg passed her up onto the lowest branch without breaking stride and followed her up into the thick cover higher up. They listened to Tilbrand searching below in amusement and moved in from the dense leaf cover to lounge on the thick branches near the trunk when he was gone.

"Why are we doing this?" Jörg whispered.

"I'm tired of everyone else's plans for me. I don't want to be a lady. I hate it. I hate sewing. I hate the long skirts. I hate sitting around. I hate everything about it."

"You like cooking," he noted.

"Gawen cooks. That's not strictly something ladies do," she countered.

"I guess. So, why this?"

"Tilbrand! Do you really want to spend the day with him lording over us? I don't."

"Sibold ordered it," Jörg rationalized.

"I'm not allowed to be a Warrior. I don't have to listen to Sibold."

"I do," he breathed, looking worried.

Regana chewed at her lower lip. "You're right. You should go back. You'll get into a lot more trouble than I will."

"Are you joking? Tilbrand will kill me. Besides, if I leave you up here in long skirts, Gawen will kill me."

"They're tucked up. I'll be fine."

His eyes lit in mischief again. "This is too much fun," he admitted.

"Good. Then we'll stay here."

"How long?"

"Forever," she replied in a wistful voice.

"We'll starve."

"Okay. Evening meal, but forever sounds better," she decided.

"Why?" Jörg asked as he changed position to face her, nestling his back to the rough trunk.

"Do you know why they want to make me a lady?"

He seemed to consider that for a long moment. "No. Not really."

"They want me to marry a Warrior," she confided, wrinkling her nose in distaste. "Can you imagine me married to Tilbrand or Wil?"

"Stand down," Jörg ordered in mock offense. "Not all Warriors are bad. I'm a Warrior. You don't seem to mind my company."

"You want to marry me?" Regana asked pointedly.

Jörg darkened. "Well...no. I don't want to marry anyone, actually."

"Neither do I."

"I know." Jörg hesitated, as if he couldn't decide how to proceed. "But, they keep telling us we have to someday." He furrowed his brow. "I have an idea."

"What?" Regana asked suspiciously. "I'm not going to a convent."

"Marry me," he teased.

"I told you, I don't want to marry anyone," she reminded him.

"Neither do I, but we have to marry someone. Why not marry a friend I can climb trees with?"

"That's not a bad plan," Regana mused.

"Give me your word," he demanded quietly.

Regana reached her knife out of her belt and sliced a shallow line down her right palm. She handed him the knife solemnly.

Jörg took it, his expression fierce. "You want to take a blood oath?" he asked. "Are you sure?"

"Why not? I can't imagine ever marrying one of those other boys." She shrugged.

He nodded and sliced his own hand. Jörg handed the knife back and clasped her palm to his own. "It's an oath," he assured her. "We marry no one but each other."

* * * *

"Gawen," Tilbrand called him in annoyance.

Gawen took in his red-faced fury in concern and darted his gaze around the training area. He cursed solidly as he made his way to the boy. "Where are they?" he asked in exasperation.

"If I knew that, they'd be here—preferably bound and gagged."

Gawen nodded in understanding. He'd considered that option on more than one occasion. "What happened?"

"They slipped into the woods and ran," he reported.

"Near my lands?"

"Yes."

"Come with me. I know where they've gone."

"How?"

"Six years of practice," Gawen spat.

Tilbrand bit back a smile at the thought. "Should I tell Sibold?" he asked seriously.

Gawen sighed. "You better. I'm sure he'll have words for them, and his presence just might save that pup from me."

When they reached Regana's tree, Tilbrand looked into the branches in confusion. "They're not up there. I already looked."

Gawen smiled and raised an eyebrow. "Regana, show yourself! If I have to come up after you..." he let the warning hang.

"Oh, Gawen," she complained. "I just wanted some peace."

"And Jörg?" he asked pointedly.

She slid into view, laid across a high limb, smiling innocently as a sprite. "I dragged him along," she admitted. "I refused to go back, and he knew you and Tilbrand would kill him if he came back without me."

"You forgot me, young lady," Sibold boomed out.

Her smile disappeared. Regana swallowed hard enough that Gawen could hear it from the ground, and Jörg appeared on a limb above her.

"We're coming down, Sibold," she assured him, dropping her legs over the edge of the branch, her skirts looped up above her knees for climbing.

Gawen started at the view she presented. He pushed Tilbrand well out of range, as she swung herself toward a lower branch. Sibold's eyes widened, and he looked away, working at words that didn't come.

"Regana, your skirts," Gawen complained.

"How else was I supposed to climb in it?" she demanded.

Sibold found his voice. "Ladies do not climb," he assured her.

"That's the problem. I am not a lady, and a lady's skirts won't change that."

"And you thought she was frightened of me," Sibold muttered to Gawen.

He didn't answer. Gawen was too busy watching the two children climb down. He saw the loop of skirt work free, but he didn't realize it was a problem until Regana tried to step down onto a lower branch. Her right foot got tangled in the hem, and her left slipped off of the branch while she tried to work it free.

At her scream of terror, Jörg's head snapped down. His eyes widened at the sight of her hanging by her hands, and he dropped to the branch he was standing on and swung himself down to hang beneath it by his knees. Gawen white-knuckled the branch just above his head, weighing his options for breaking her fall.

Jörg grabbed her wrists. "Regana, look at me," he ordered.

She met his eyes, shaking in fear.

"Can you work your foot free?"

Regana shook her head. "It's stuck fast," she decided miserably.

"If I lift you to the branch above, can you straddle it and hold on?"

"I think so."

"We'll do that then." Jörg lifted her easily and turned Regana to help her over the limb. "One hand at a time," he told her, releasing one and waiting for her to grip the branch before releasing the other wrist. "Sit still. I'm coming down to you."

Jörg grabbed the branch his legs were on and lowered himself behind her smoothly. While the two older men watched, he leaned around her to work the skirt free from her foot. He looped it back into her belt and tucked it in firmly. "Can you climb down, now?" he asked.

"Not in this," she replied, obviously shaken.

Jörg nodded. "I'll get you down." He stood on the limb and stepped around her carefully before lowering himself in front of Regana with his back to her. "Wrap your arms and legs around me," he instructed.

"What?" she asked in confusion.

"Either you climb or you hold on and I carry you. Which is it?"

She hesitated for just a moment before wrapping her arms around his shoulders and her legs around his waist. "I'm ready," Regana told him, burying her face in his back.

Jörg swung down the remaining branches easily, even with Regana's added weight. On the ground, he faced Gawen and swallowed hard. "If you're going to strike me, please take Regana off first," he requested. "I'll take the punishment. Just don't place her in the middle."

Gawen took Regana from him, shaking so badly that he could barely stand. He let down her skirts while she clung to him. "Regana, I have never hit you in anger," he began.

"If you're going to, I accept it," she breathed.

"Not this time. I think you've suffered enough, but if you ever do it again..." he warned.

"I won't."

"Are you all right?"

"I'm fine." Her voice sounded of exhaustion.

She started to back away, but he grasped her hand. Regana wrenched it back and fisted it in her skirts.

"You're bleeding."

"It's fine, Gawen," she insisted.

"Let me see it," he demanded gruffly.

Regana hesitated, sighing before she opened her palm for his inspection. The cut was from a blade, not from tree bark. Gawen flicked a glance at Jörg suspiciously and noted that he had his hand fisted, too.

"What was the blood oath you took?" he asked.

Regana bit her lower lip for a moment. "Blood oaths are between the two people alone," she informed him.

Gawen glared at her, then slid his gaze to Jörg. "Well?" he demanded, making no effort to hide the threat woven into his tone.

Regana flashed Jörg a pleading look.

The boy darkened. "It is between us alone," he repeated.

"Jörg," Sibold barked.

He winced. "I'm sorry, Sibold. I gave my word. Honor demands that I stand by it now."

"Then honor has cost you extra duties. In the future, do not make pledges that will contradict your position."

"Yes, Sibold," he breathed miserably.

Regana grimaced. "I'm sorry, Jörg. I keep getting you into trouble."

"Don't apologize." He smiled a secretive smile. "Just remember that oath."

She smiled widely, and her eyes glowed in mischief. "Should I?"

"You had best remember it. It was a blood oath, and it was your idea. You're honor bound to it now."

Her smile disappeared. "You planned this?" she half-asked, half-accused.

"Yes, I did," he admitted happily.

"You sneak," she shot at him.

Jörg offered a comic bow and walked away with a smug smile on his face and Tilbrand in his wake.

Regana fumed, mumbling curses at his retreating back.

"What was the oath, Regana?" Gawen demanded.

"Nothing he'll survive long enough to collect."

"Now, my dear," Sibold chided her. "Is that ladylike?"

"Who cares?" she grumbled. "I'll never be a lady."

Chapter One

500 AD

Jörg swept Regana into his arms the moment she entered his chambers, stifling her laughter with a passionate kiss. He carried her to the furs before the roaring fire and deposited her gently on her feet. "Undress for me," he requested in a voice rough with his need.

She smiled, no doubt in the knowledge of what the simple pleasure of seeing her disrobe did to him. Her movements had ceased to be tentative weeks ago, and the woman left was nothing but sensuous and bold. That, as much as her body, had him aching long before he took her every night she came to him.

Disrobed and with her black hair cascading around her hips in silken waves, she reached her hands out to him in invitation. Regana was one of a kind, a rare jewel. She looked and acted like no other woman he'd met. Some of the villagers considered her a bad omen, but Jörg could see nothing bad about her.

Jörg groaned in anticipation as he took her mouth fiercely and drew a hand from her hip up to capture the full swell of her breast. "All I can think about when you're not with me is this," he breathed as he swept her down onto the furs with him and covered her with his body.

"I've noticed," she teased, running her hand over the bruise on his shoulder. "Gawen will not be kind if you let your attention wander again."

"Neither will Sibold, but enough of them. I want you."

"Good," she purred, moving against him purposefully.

"Tell me," he requested.

"I am yours, Jörg."

"You will marry me when the battle is over?"

"As soon as it is allowed. You are permitted your choice then, and Gawen must agree. He will be so intent on Bavin, he won't care about anything else." She smiled widely. "Besides, we have a blood oath," she reminded him.

Jörg chuckled. "All that time, you complained that I tricked you to it, and now you throw it back at me," he mused.

"You did, but maybe I wanted to be tricked."

She was suddenly very subdued.

Jörg tried to meet her eyes. "Regana?"

She smiled weakly. "I only fear that the others will learn about us. If they do, Gawen will kill you. You know he will."

Jörg sighed raggedly. "If I don't have you, I die anyway."

He knew that was true. Jörg had fought off the fire in his blood for months before he gave in. Sibold had warned them about this part of the curse. With the speed, increased healing, reaction time, and *Blutjagd*—the thirst for the fight—came the sexual burn, the urge to choose a mate.

Sibold had decreed that none could make that choice until after the battle, to maximize their *Blutjagd* in battle he was sure, but Jörg couldn't wait. The want had burned at him until he'd felt he was going insane. He'd felt himself printing and had been powerless to stop it. After that, Jörg had been tortured until he'd consummated the union with Regana. Other women had ceased to be a comfort long before that time, though he still occasionally performed with one to this day—with Regana's blessing—so that no one would get suspicious.

It surprised him that she'd accepted him so readily. In retrospect, Jörg wondered if the *Fluch*—the curse—had helped in that respect somehow. Regana, though not the meek flower many in the village painted her, was still proper and fine, having left her tree climbing and hunting days far behind. Still she'd reacted to his first, admittedly skirting the edges of brutal, advances so readily that he'd rationalized later that the *Fluch* could only be to blame for her response somehow. He'd rationalized that much later—after she'd succumbed to him, after Jörg had taken her several times without even the benefit of shelter, after she'd started coming to his chamber to meet him, once his mind had formed a truce with the fire that consumed him any night Regana did not come to lie with him.

As he moved his hands over her, drawing her into a need that would have her ready for his invasion in mere moments, Jörg considered his situation. He had given up his life the first time he'd touched her, with that first demanding kiss that he stole from her beneath their tree that had rolled over into his first possession of her with hardly a breath between.

To this day, Jörg was not entirely sure what happened in those fevered moments between meeting her eyes and taking her on the cool grass, but once embarked upon, it was a course he could never turn from. Some part of him wasn't sure, even now, that

Regana had admitted her willingness to the course, but she had been willing. He knew that much, and the knowledge had saved his soul and his life.

In that pivotal moment, Jörg had broken the rules of training. Until he earned his seal and was granted his autonomy, he was at Sibold's whim, and Sibold would not be sparing in his death if he learned of this trespass.

Worse, he'd taken...and continued to take Regana, a Schwertträger woman. Her father was dead, but even were he not, by virtue of Gawen's place as first-cursed and having completed his training, he was lord of the house. By all rights, Jörg's life was forfeit to Gawen alone if they were caught. *Blutjagd* upon him, Gawen would demand Jörg's life when he could show mercy and be content with a beating for the trespass.

Even if Gawen did show mercy, Sibold would not. If they were caught, Jörg would die by someone's hand within the hour.

Regana moaned beneath him and arched to his caresses. His blood screamed for release, and he moved to take her, shuddering in pleasure as he thrust into her. Jörg took her fast and hard.

He argued with himself often that he'd like to take her slowly, but in the heat of the moment, he had no control. A part of him feared that he never would know such control with Regana, even when they gained the leisure of time for such pursuits. It was probably a good thing that she reveled in this type of passion.

It would be over soon, the midnight meeting and hiding. The battle was less than a week off. Once they returned victorious, he could claim her openly, properly. His duty completed, Jörg would reap his reward. He would have his wife and children. He would live a life of ease, until duty called him again.

Jörg roared out his release to the empty house around them, too empty since his mother had died, wrapping himself protectively around her. *Anything for Regana!* He would go into battle and face the gates of hell itself for her—and he might. They were outnumbered more than ten to one, but the *Fluch* allowed them the ability to defeat many more than that.

"More than human," he could hear Sibold quote in his mind.

Jörg shuddered at the thought. Faster and stronger, yes. But in many ways, the Warriors were less than human now. They were vicious, predatory, territorial, rutting animals that were only stable killing or training to do so and lying with a woman. Regana was his salvation and his life.

He held her close to him as long as she would allow and groaned in pleasure as she kissed his blood mark tenderly. Finally, she planted a kiss on his cheek and rose to collect her dress. She donned it quickly and pulled on her cloak against the chill of the night. As always, it was Regana who saw the truth that she must leave before they were discovered together. Left to Jörg, they would have been found in each other's arms at daybreak long ago.

"I live for the night you don't have to leave," he told her yet again. It was an old refrain, but no less true. The idea of having her in his bed all night... To have her again and again *in* a night was his idea of paradise.

Regana smiled patiently. "Then make your choice of me as soon as the battle ends," she teased. "Tell them you've printed so far that you cannot wait for the ceremony. By the while, I must go before Gawen finds me gone."

"Take care, *Geliebte*," he called after her as she left. Jörg smiled at the small endearment. Regana had always been his beloved. She would always be his only beloved.

Jörg sighed as the door closed behind her. He stretched out on the furs and drank in the heat of the fire. It didn't warm him as much as Regana did, but until she was in his arms again, it would be his only comfort.

Something intruded on his senses, and he furrowed his brow. Jörg couldn't identify it readily, save its obvious malice, and he sat up, grasping for his weapons.

The blow to his head sent him sprawling over the drawn blade, and he vaguely felt it cut into his arm as he landed unceremoniously on the furs. A shadowy figure crossed the blurry brightness of the fire; then the darkness took him.

* * * *

"You hit him too hard!"

Jörg tried to place the disembodied voice that intruded on his slumber.

Bertolf? But why would his cursed brothers...

His heart sank. *Regana!* They had seen her leave his home and had taken him to face Gawen. He would die very shortly.

"Sunrise is coming soon. We can't hide him all day," Geldric complained miserably.

Hide me? Why would they bother to hide me? Jörg's death would be a very public display.

A hand touched his neck, cold and somehow menacing even in its regard for his well being. "Be calm. He wakes," Tilbrand ordered the other men. The hand retreated, then smacked his cheek roughly. "Wake, Jörg. Face us."

Jörg forced his eyelids up and squinted in the dim light of the training area. He groaned at the spike of pain that split his head in two and scanned his eyes over the men assembled around him: Dado, Redulf, Bertolf, Geldric, and Tilbrand. "Where is Gawen?" he managed in a thick, confused voice.

"Are you so anxious to face him, Jörg?" Tilbrand asked in amusement.

"I don't understand," he moaned, trying to find some sense in what they were saying.

He would have no choice in facing Gawen. Surely, even now, the older Warrior was being dragged from his bed to come deal with the trespass to his house. Would Gawen strike Regana for her part in it? The thought hurt. He could do that, and in his fury, Gawen might do it.

"No one has informed Gawen...yet."

Jörg looked at them in apprehension for the first time. "My penalty is in Gawen's hands alone," he reminded them. They couldn't plan on taking the penalty themselves. The censure to them would be even higher than the censure to Jörg in its wake. They would overstep their bounds if they did so.

"We don't dispute that. We don't wish you to die, Jörg." Tilbrand said it smoothly, too calmly for the younger man's comfort. "We understand the fire in your soul for her. You are the greatest of us. It is only right that the one who burns brightest in battle is consumed in other ways as well."

"Then, why have you done this?" he asked in confusion.

"We need your help."

"In battle? Of course. If this is a warning to control the fire until after the battle, I understand."

The mixture of amusement and unease on the assembled faces set his teeth on edge. This was no simple warning. Jörg wasn't sure he was comfortable with whatever it was at this point.

"We need you for another reason, Jörg. We need you to remove the Stone for us."

"You can't," he protested. "Sibold's magic protects the Stone from those who would use it selfishly."

"Yes, it does," Tilbrand spat. "We cannot remove it. Only one who removes it with no intent of using its power selfishly can do so."

"Why would I do that?" he asked weakly, suddenly shivering in the cold room, exposed before the older men in all, body and soul. "Why would you?"

"To be victorious," Geldric replied as if it should have been obvious.

"To be immortal," Redulf added. "I have no wish to die in battle."

Jörg could see the fear in his eyes. They'd had no choice in their cursed state. They were born to it, and Redulf wanted no part of it.

"Immortality without your soul?" Jörg asked in disbelief. "You've gone mad. Why should I do this? I would rather give my life to Gawen than free the Stone to you. That aside, pulling the Stone to save my life from Gawen's blade...or even Sibold's would be a selfish act. The Stone will not release to me."

He smiled at his victory, but his smile faded as Tilbrand threw back his head and laughed into the semi-darkness, a wild, frightening sound. At twenty-three, the only older first-cursed was Gawen himself. Tilbrand was a huge bear of a man, and Jörg suddenly felt small and defenseless. The older man's eyes were cold as the winter ice and friendly as a forged iron blade as he leaned over his prey.

"If that was your reason, you'd be right," he assured Jörg. "You will not remove the Stone to save your own life. That would be selfish. I agree."

Jörg couldn't find his voice. A sick certainty cut through his heart like the slice of a weapon. He met those cold eyes again.

"You will take it for the most unselfish reason of all, to save an innocent woman." His smile turned licentious. "Well...not so innocent after all, as we've all seen," Tilbrand decided. "Very well, in fact."

Jörg launched at the larger man, pitting his sixteen years of pure fury at the comparative giant. "You won't touch her," he growled out, feeling his blood burn in *Blutjagd*. For the defense of his mate, Jörg could take the life of one who threatened her without a single thought to the contrary.

Had his only opponent been Tilbrand, Jörg had no doubts that the older man would be dead at his feet in short order. He roared in rage, as four more pairs of hands removed him bodily from his enemy's throat. Had they been human and not cursed as he was, Jörg would have easily killed them all in defense of Regana, even unarmed as he was.

As it was, it was difficult for them to hold and subdue him. It took uncounted heavy blows to slow him and a sacred weapon at his throat to still his fight. Tilbrand administered one final, crushing blow to his already broken ribs in retribution, and Jörg spit blood at his foe.

"You're right," Tilbrand panted at him. "I won't touch her. I'll turn her over to Gawen. If the sun rises and the Stone is not in my hand, I will kill you. I will tell Gawen that you lost your mind because she baited you, breaking our laws and forcing you to print while you trained. With the battle so close, the villagers will demand her death."

"Kill me," he groaned. "Gawen may do many things, but he will not take her life. I know he won't. You can explain my death. How will you explain hers?"

"He will take her life, if I speak for it," another voice asserted.

Jörg squinted into the deep shadows. "Marclef?" he asked in disbelief. "You cannot approve of this." Surely, the young leader who'd taken over when Eberhard was aging could not think to endorse this course of action.

"I give it my full support. I will not lose my village."

Jörg groaned and shook his head. "You will not lose it. We can handle twice as many as we are."

"I can't wager that. We cannot lose."

"Why, Tilbrand? What do you get in exchange for your soul?"

"I'll be a god," he decided. "Is there any greater thing?"

"You'll be an outcast," he shot back. "You will lose all."

"No," Marclef assured him. "Ensure my victory, and I'll ensure your place. You'll retain all your rights, as long as you take your blood elsewhere. You have my word."

"You don't believe that, do you?" Jörg searched the faces of the men around him, finding acceptance or mild discomfort but no doubt. They couldn't be that blind! "Our brothers will hunt you. Our people will fear and hate you. Better an honorable death," he told Tilbrand.

"Will Regana's death be honorable?" Tilbrand asked, prompting Jörg to surge against the hands that held him fast. "With the five of us and Marclef speaking against her, she will face a very painful death. Can you let her die for you as you would die for her?"

Jörg closed his eyes. He prayed that Sibold and Gawen would not allow such a thing. "I die without her," he breathed. "I lose her either way."

They could do it, he realized. They could take Regana's life, if the outcry from the villagers were strong enough. Could he let her die if he could stop it? But life without her, even a damned life, would be intolerable, and Jörg would be releasing the worst of evils on the world to save her.

"Touch the Stone and lose all kind feelings," Dado whispered close to his ear. "She will live, and you will not miss what you have lost. If you find being damned so unbearable, kill yourself after your duty at the battle, but by the gods, save her life by losing yours...if you love her."

Jörg cried out his loss, feeling the mounting madness as if Regana lay dead at his feet. If he did this, he would be dead to her. "Loose me," he ground out dangerously. "You'll have your Stone. Damn you all for wanting it, and damn me for providing it to you. And you!" He looked at Tilbrand. "You will pay for this before I die, and if you ever lay hands on her, I will make it the most painful death I can."

"As you wish," he answered confidently. "Get me the Stone, and you may have any boon you wish, except my life. That I will not grant you."

The hands released him suddenly, and Jörg took to his feet with a feral look at Tilbrand and then Marclef. "Do not think your dogs will protect you from me," he warned the leader as he stalked to the Stone. They would both pay for making him lose his chosen one...Regana, who was to save his soul. Now, he was giving it away to save her life.

He stared miserably at the blood red stone, black and forbidding in the dim light. His soul was forfeit now—or would be in a few short moments.

Please, if you have any mercy, do not let Regana die at their hands. Let me protect her somehow. He begged that one boon of the gods, sure that they weren't listening already, that his choice had damned him before the action sealed his fate.

His hand closed around the Stone, and Jörg sucked in his breath at the surge of power that rushed in his veins. The Stone lit up with a fire from within, and he saw the blue flaw in its depths clearly in the deep red light that encompassed it. As the power built within him, the flaw spiraled before his eyes, expanding until it loomed like a great beast before him: two arrows crossed over a bow, Jäger seal.

A voice whispered and echoed in his mind. "Only in death are you free. Your wish is granted."

He cried out in anguish as he felt himself falling through space and time, absorbing information as stars spiraled past him, burning him until Jörg felt he would turn to ash where he stood.

Darkness closed around him.

Jörg opened his eyes and stared at the rough stone ceiling in a numb detachment, unsure of how he came to be lying boneless on the floor. *So, this is what it's like to be emotionless. Thank the gods, I won't feel.*

He considered using his newfound powers against the others before they could claim the Stone's power for themselves, but he lacked the ability to even control his limbs. He was powerless as Tilbrand pried the Stone from his hand.

Jörg looked at the glee evident on the older man's face in a mixture of rage and hate. *I can feel.*

No kinder emotions, he reminded himself. He could still feel the darker emotions.

Loss. I feel my loss keenly...sadness, pain. Regana, what have I done? A tear wound down his cheek.

He felt it as Tilbrand and the others joined him in damnation. Jörg saw the flaw reveal itself to each of them in turn. Tilbrand saw the tipped cross and wolf head of the Lord Kreuzträger. Redulf, Bertolf, and Geldric saw a general Kreuzträger seal—not the lord's seal, but there were no others but its lord now. Dado saw the seals of Jäger and Kreuzträger combined and topped by a symbol on no one's seal, a crown.

Jörg stifled a sob, recalling that the seal revealed to him was not a lord's seal either. His death would be at the hands of a Warrior of Jäger, but not her lord. He would live with his loss far longer than he cared to think about, at least seventeen years until a Jäger heir was birthed and first nighted.

The voice that had addressed him, addressed each of the others in their turn, naming them and warning them of the humanity they'd lost. No longer worthy of their human names, Tilbrand was Resten, Dado was Lorian, Redulf was Carstol, Bertolf was Draden, and Geldric was Cerran, the names of the fallen gods cast out after waging war on the Warrior's paradise. But no name had been provided for Jörg himself and no warning of what he'd lost.

Perhaps, it was unnecessary. Jörg knew what he'd lost. Perhaps, he no longer deserved a name, at all.

Recovered once all were changed, Jörg faced them in a rage. "You have your names and your damnation," he spat. "Enjoy it until your end comes for you."

Bertolf—*Draden,* he reminded himself—approached warily. "What are you?" he asked. "Why can I not sense you like I can the others? What is your name? What is your fate? Why are you apart from us?"

Jörg's face broke into a broad smile. "I am not like you," he mused. "I see all, because mine was a selfless act. I am Jörg, and my fate is to live long. The gods knew my intent when I touched the Stone. I am damned but not as damned as you."

Resten charged at him with his sacred weapon in hand, and Jörg read his intent to slay his enemy clearly. Even before the flood of information in his mind assured him that this was not possible on many levels, Jörg had dematerialized. Resten barreled through where the younger beast stood only a moment before, encountering only air behind his swing. When Jörg materialized again, he did so clothed and cocky.

Resten whirled to face him. "How?" he demanded.

"I have been gifted knowledge you are denied. You will have to learn it for yourself. Dawn approaches, and I must go to ground. Don't despair. Your beasts will keep you alive to see another night. It pleases them to have you as their homes. Leave your weapons. You may no longer use them. We are all unworthy to take life that way now."

Jörg dematerialized with a horrible, mad laugh that he could hardly identify as his own voice and raced away on the breeze.

He sobbed as he looked at the cool earth. Despite his knowledge, the idea of dematerializing and sinking deep within the damp dirt beneath him filled him with dread.

Fear, another emotion I wish I didn't have but one useful in controlling my errant brothers.

Being disembodied was disconcerting. Still, the sun was approaching and being damned aside, Jörg could not leave this life until he was sure Regana was safe.

Miserably, he sank into the waiting soil. The soil would heal the wounds the others had inflicted on him, all but one wound. That one would be with him for the rest of his days, until some Warrior *Jäger geboren* released him. Jörg would not be permitted to die any other way. He knew that now. The beast inside him would make him seek survival at all costs, until his life was honestly taken by the right Warrior.

Jörg felt a rush of satisfaction and amusement as the others were forcibly dematerialized and dragged beneath the ground wherever they had staggered to in the short time since their change. He felt an almost savage glee that Resten burned momentarily before his pain forced him to stop fighting his beast. Resten feared this part of their existence most of all. That could prove a most useful bit of information when it came time to call in his revenge.

Chapter Two

"How could they?" Gawen demanded.

Pauwel cringed inwardly at the explosion of his temper. At twenty-five, five years Pauwel's senior, he'd assumed Schwertträger was above such outbursts.

"We knew this was a possibility when there were so many born," Sibold sighed, showing his age for the first time that Pauwel could remember.

"But the magic on the bloodstone... How could they get past it?" Gawen continued, making his demand more specific. "It cannot be taken selfishly."

"You are right. You see the weapons left here? They are only of the five older men."

"What of Jörg?" Ditrich demanded. "As a beast, he cannot wield them. Or have they killed him?"

"No," Sibold assured him. "He lives as a beast. The Stone confirms that. I had already checked their chambers before I sent for you. Jörg was brought here by force. There is no doubt of that. He was injured and dragged from his bed. Once here, he removed the Stone for them."

"Still," Pauwel countered, "he would have to be willing to touch the Stone, not simply to save his own life."

"He was. He did. He removed it for them willingly but unselfishly. I don't understand it. The Stone speaks to me, but it is frustrating in what it does not say.

"And it makes no difference why Jörg touched the Stone. The beasts are free now. As the Stone demands, our curse is now permanent. Until the final beast is freed, you stand charged, as do your descendents. It is the price you were born to. Our futures are linked. Neither can be free without freeing the other."

Wil grunted his agreement. "Then we finish them quickly, before they are set in their new power," he decided.

"No," Marclef exploded.

Pauwel rolled his eyes. Leader or not, this was not Marclef's concern. It was the concern of the Warriors.

"We have few enough Warriors left to us. We cannot risk losing the rest of you—or even some of you, before our enemies are vanquished. After the battle, there will be time enough to hunt them."

Sibold sighed bitterly. "It is not the worst plan," he admitted. "Training will be required. Fighting beasts is much different than fighting humans. A killing blow to a human may not even slow a beast."

All heads came up, as the door swung open and someone rushed in. Pauwel strained his neck to see over and around the crowd, and his breath caught as he saw Regana...pale, jittery and out of breath, at the edge of the training area.

"Is it true?" she demanded in a shaky voice.

Gawen scowled at her. "Go home, Regana. You cannot be here now. This is a time for the men."

Pauwel looked at him in shock. Never had there been a time that Regana had not been welcome in their midst.

"Is it true?" she asked in a more urgent tone.

"Yes," Gawen snapped at her. "Now, go! We will discuss this at home."

She scanned the faces of the assembled men in a sort of shock and disbelief, making a list of her lost brothers no doubt.

"Regana!"

She met her brother's eyes miserably and turned away. The door closed with much more force than Pauwel thought possible for a woman her size.

Pauwel dragged his gaze away painfully. He knew Regana was his chosen. He had known it forever, it seemed. Seeing her upset made him ache and his blood burn to avenge the hurt, but touching her would mean death or madness, madness if he didn't claim her for his own and death if he did. He tried to attend to the conversation, though his attention kept wandering to the door she'd left by and his mind to the lady herself.

"What was that all about?" Cunczel demanded.

Gawen sighed. "She and Jörg played together as children, as you well remember. She still sees him as a beloved brother. It will be very hard for her to think him capable of what he has done."

Pauwel fisted his hand behind the cover of his back, feeling the bones shift and his nails cut flesh. As if Jörg's betrayal was not enough alone, he had hurt Regana in doing it. Pauwel seethed at the thoughtlessness of the beast Jörg was before he turned truly beast.

* * * *

Regana veered off the main trail and into the woods that separated her family's land from Jörg's. No, she reminded herself, not Jörg's anymore. His lands and possessions were forfeit now. As the last of his line, they could not even be passed to a younger brother or to a married sister.

She pushed the thought away before she could follow it to its painful conclusion. Regana rushed past the cold, empty house and all its memories of demanding, unrestrained lovemaking before the fire in his chambers...all promises broken. That was a place of lies. He'd dared ask for her promise to marry just before he betrayed all! How could he make love to her and make promises to her if he planned this?

She collapsed at the base of the tree she and Jörg had played under as children. Nine years older, Gawen had been more a young adult than a playmate. He'd rarely come here unless it was to drag them to their homes. He'd never played here with them. It was a place for them alone.

At the time, it had seemed so right that the first few times Jörg took her, he took her here, beneath the branches that had sheltered and protected them all their lives. Maybe it had been right then. Regana couldn't help but believe that Jörg had been honest when it all began. She knew that he hadn't been lying then. He couldn't have been.

He'd touched her in ways she'd never imagined were possible. He'd kissed her and taken her with a fierce passion she'd never dreamed existed before Jörg made his intentions clear to her. Could a man... Could *Jörg* touch her and show love in such a way and not be utterly sincere?

Regana curled her cheek into the grass and let the tears fall. "Damn him," she hitched. Her tears intensified in the realization that he had taken care of that step by his own hand. He'd left her. Jörg had convinced her he wanted her as his chosen, then he'd left her. Why would he do that?

There were only two possibilities that came to mind. In the first, Jörg had been tricked into what he did. She'd like to believe that, though she realized how unlikely it was.

The second frightened her. If he did it willingly, Jörg had used her with no intention of ever choosing her. Regana fisted her hand in the new grass as the full force of that thought assaulted her.

When she was cried out, she lay for a long time in their place, saying a strange sort of goodbye to her hopes and dreams. Regana could not say goodbye to Jörg, until she knew for sure that he had done the horrible things he stood accused of. If he hadn't done them—

Still, he was lost to her for all time.

* * * *

Gawen felt as if the very life had been dragged from him. The entire day had been spent arguing. The Stone spoke to Sibold in the strange way it did with its chosen keeper. It had named the beasts that inhabited their former brothers—all but Jörg. The Stone had named him not at all. In the end, Sibold was still confused by that, so he'd named the beast himself. For all intents and purposes, Jörg was now Veriel, the Mad Deceiver. It seemed fitting, considering the circumstances.

Marclef had a twisted view of their priorities. He couldn't see past the approaching enemy. Oblivious to the fact that a much smaller complement with much more potential for destruction existed, he seemed to be doggedly ignoring the larger threat in favor of the smaller.

On some things, Sibold agreed with him, like waiting to attack the beasts. On others, it became a battle between the man responsible for the people's livelihood and the Warrior responsible for their security. Everyone present knew that Sibold was the person operating in his own bailiwick, but Marclef was popular and powerful in his own right and held the threat of wielding that power to make their duty difficult over them. On some issues, Sibold had accepted the smaller man's ridiculous bullying to shut him up.

The thing that worried the young Warriors the most was the change Marclef had demanded in the choosing. Originally, all fifteen of the marriageable young ladies had agreed to stand a panel, accepting whatever Warrior chose them for printing. Only in the case that two Warriors chose the same woman would mediation by the leader and Sibold be required. The woman's preference would be considered, since she would suddenly be in a position to have a preference and thus to be unwilling with one or the other, but the relative needs of the Warriors would be paramount, and the ladies understood that. A Warrior too far printed could not change course lest he go insane. As it was, any man in the throes of printing, even early printing, would experience excruciating pain at the loss of his proposed chosen mate.

Marclef had demanded to set aside the original agreement. He'd argued that the women had agreed to wed men whose curse would end with them and give birth to fully human children to husbands who may, as any *Soldat*, be called to fight again for the village.

What they would be agreeing to now would be very different. They would be marrying into a cursed line and producing cursed children of men who would be doomed to prowl the night to hunt down vicious beasts. Marclef proposed to ask each woman to reconsider her participation, based on the new situation.

That proclamation had raised a riot among the Warriors. They had persevered the waiting, upheld their half of the arrangement, based on the participation of the whole group of fifteen women. The possibility of beasts had never been a secret.

What if more than eight of them pulled out, leaving one or more of the Warriors without a chosen mate? Not only would the future of fighting the beasts be weaker, but the unwed Warriors would eventually go mad and have to be put to death.

In addition, there was the unspoken concern many of them shared. As Gawen craved Bavin, several of the other men had developed a longing for a favorite—had, in effect, made their choices without benefit of claiming the woman in any way. Sibold knew it. They all knew it.

Ditrich favored Anabilia. Pauwel had the look of a man fallen, but he kept the woman's identity deeply hidden. Unlike the others who gave indication that their hearts were lost, he never gave a hint of the woman who'd caught his eye. If any of those women changed their minds... It was a death sentence for the man too far printed. All in all, this announcement was not what the Warriors needed with beasts underfoot and the battle looming.

On the other hand, the importance of the Warriors established, they had been granted their seals to protect their families in this time of need. The Lords of Jäger, Kreuzträger, Schwertträger, Schmied, Landwirt, Kaufmann, and Maher had taken their places as true lord Warriors. Sibold had looked at the seals of their opposite numbers sadly before locking them away.

Gawen sighed as his home came into view. Now he had to deal with Regana.

He slipped through the door and took in the sight of his younger sister. Her hair was pulled back in a hasty thong behind her head, and she had obviously spent a great deal of time crying. Her eyes were puffy and red, and her cheeks were enflamed. She cooked frantically, a sure sign that she'd come to no accord with her emotions.

As always when Regana was so upset, it tore his heart from his chest to see it. Gawen would do anything to make it right for her, but this time, he was at a loss.

"Regana," he soothed her.

"I don't want to talk about it," she warned him.

"I'm sorry I snapped at you. I was upset."

"Apology accepted." She pushed past him in annoyance.

"Please, tell me what's wrong."

She looked at him in disbelief. "Everything is wrong," she exploded, as she chopped roots into the stew she was working on without looking at them. Her hands were shaking so badly that he was afraid she would take her finger instead of the food.

He reached for her hand to remove the knife, but she jerked away. Cursing himself, Gawen gripped her wrist and pried the knife from her fingers. Regana glared at him, and he released her wrist, keeping the knife from her.

"Now, if you're concerned about the beasts, don't be. We can handle them. It has happened before, in ancient times."

"I'm sure you will, Gawen," she answered sarcastically.

Regana started to walk away, but he took her by the arm and led her to a chair. She sat, looking uncomfortable and tense.

"I can't help you, if you won't explain," he informed her calmly.

"There's nothing to explain," she protested.

"If this is about Jörg—"

Regana shot him a seething glare that stopped him cold. "I told you I don't want to discuss it. My friend is a traitor, and he is gone. His holdings are forfeit. What more is there to say, Gawen?"

He sighed raggedly. "I know you're upset—"

"Upset?" she stormed. "Upset doesn't even begin to cover what I'm feeling right now."

"Should I retreat now and try again when you're calmer?" he asked in exasperation.

"Retreat for all time. I never want to hear his name again," she finished miserably.

Gawen sighed. "As you wish. There is one thing we must discuss."

"And that is?"

"This." Gawen dangled an amulet before her eyes. "The beasts are loose. You must be protected. All the lords are protecting their families now."

"You're a lord." She said it evenly, sadly, and Gawen could almost hear the statement in her mind that Jörg could have been a lord, too. Instead, he chose damnation.

"Yes, and I must do this."

"I don't want it," she decided.

"What?" he stormed. "Why not?"

"It's bad enough that you're my lord now. That...thing means you own me. I won't stand for it."

"It means nothing but that the beasts cannot touch you."

She shot him a look of mistrust.

"Nothing has changed."

"Everything has changed," she muttered.

"I have no more power over you than I ever had." Gawen ground his teeth. He had little enough, as it was. "Yes, I have to approve a marriage for you, but if you are content to wed, I would not stand in your way. You know that."

She snorted and rolled her eyes rudely. "As if either of us have a choice in that."

"You do now," he informed her. "Marclef has decreed that any woman who so chooses may rescind her vow. None of you will be forced to wed the Warriors. If you choose to keep to your vow, you will abide by the rules of choosing. If not, you are freed."

Gawen felt his heart sink. If Regana pulled out, Sibold would be most put out. He had always claimed that the Stone intended for her to be a lady to one of the young lords. He would not take it lightly if she balked him now. Still, it was not within either of their power to demand this of her. If she was unwilling, nothing could be done about it.

Regana looked at him in shock. "Is it really that simple? Say the word, and I am free?"

"Yes. The Warriors are furious, but Marclef has the right to make that declaration."

She met his eyes sadly. "Then, I am not taking part in the choosing. I will not marry a Warrior. I may never marry, if such is my choice."

"If this is about—"

"It's not," she shot back, cutting him off cleanly.

"Will you wear the amulet?"

"As you wish," she conceded.

Gawen settled the amulet around her neck and recited the ancient blessing. "*Durch die Götter, die uns alle schmiedeten, bewillige ich Ihnen den Schutz der HausSchwertträger Irgendwelche und die ganze unsere Art und Stämme legen das Leben nieder, um Ihr vom Übel zu Konservieren, das unter uns geht. Weg jetzt gesegnet unter uns.*" He sealed the blessing by brushing his lips over her forehead.

Regana nodded quietly. "May I continue cooking now, Gawen?"

"In a moment. Why have you removed yourself from the choosing?"

"Because, it is my right to do so," she countered smoothly.

"Did Jörg make some promise I should know about?"

"Jörg? He was a hopeless child who is now a beast. I don't want to discuss him."

"Then why?" he prodded.

"Because, I will not marry a Warrior. Not now. Not ever," she promised.

"Because they must fight the beasts?"

"That's not reason enough?" she inquired in disbelief.

Gawen sighed. "I hope you'll reconsider. You can, anytime you like."

"I won't," Regana decided. She snatched her knife away and went back to cooking.

* * * *

Jörg materialized well after nightfall. He was so miserable that he couldn't even find amusement in the clumsy attempts his damned brethren made at the job.

His first duty after materializing was speeding off into the night to check the progress of the enemy approaching. That done, he had no problems tracking the others.

Resten sneered, as Jörg materialized in their midst. "What do you want?" he growled.

"Do you intend to keep your word?" he asked. "Will you fight to keep your place?"

"I thought you believed the promise was a lie," Carstol shot back miserably.

"I still do. I fight because I gave my word when I started training. I asked if you intended to do it."

Cerran nodded. "It is our only hope of peace. We must."

"Good. If you start out now, you can reach them in three days walking speed for you, since you know no other way of travel." He grinned. "Perhaps, four for all of you. That will give you several nights to experiment

53

with killing lone soldiers before the main battle. Your beasts will help you learn."

"How could you know that?" Draden asked.

"I have just returned from scouting their location."

"How?" Resten demanded. "Tell us how you move."

"Ask your beast. You wanted it. Learn from it, if you dare. I have what I need."

"Will you come with us?" Lorian asked in his quiet way.

"I will be there for the battle, and to lead you to the battle. I can find you when I have need to find you." A cold smile touched his lips. "Why should I be uncomfortable until then?" He looked to the sky and took a deep breath of the night air. "You should go now. The moon is already high."

He dematerialized smoothly and stayed to hear them cursing him, cursing themselves and their choice, and deciding to go. The others had no sense of him, and for that Jörg was glad. It gave him yet another advantage that they could never know when he watched them unless he wished it, even if he didn't expend the energy required to hide himself from the Warriors.

They left, still cursing their inability to utilize the immense power they had chosen. They needed the practice, and they knew it. If Jörg was lucky, they might even get themselves seriously injured enough to send them to ground for several days and make them easier for the Warriors to pick off at the battle. Of course, Resten was the only one he could hope to rid himself of that way, he realized. He was the only one who'd seen a lord's seal in the Stone.

On the other hand, if the beasts succeeded in their learning, it would only be the enemy they were killing off. Overall, killing off the incoming forces was a good plan, no matter how it was accomplished.

Jörg sped over the countryside to Schwertträger lands. His heart sank as he looked at the house. It had once been his second home, where he'd chased Regana through the rooms while she'd squealed in delight.

Everything was different now. Gawen, who he had once considered a brother, was his mortal enemy. Regana was lost to him. Even if she didn't turn from him, he had nothing to offer her now. Jörg had no kind emotions to spend on her. He couldn't give her children and be a husband to her, as she deserved. He pushed away the pain that ate at him, the loss he would always bear.

He should have realized when he chose a place to go to ground that Regana would come there in her pain and grief as well. Her time there had been torture for him. Disembodied, Jörg hadn't been able to touch her, to hold her as she deserved.

If he could have chosen death at that moment just to hold her and ease her pain, he would have. But, he couldn't. Being damned had closed that door to him. Jörg could not choose death now. In addition, no matter what pain his continued existence cost her or himself, Jörg couldn't die if he knew that there was any possibility that Regana needed him.

Still, as Jörg lay below, he had heard her cursing him, and it hurt in a way he hadn't realized he could hurt. Worse, Regana believed his love was a lie...or that it had become a lie at some point. He could imagine the salt of her tears as they mixed with the soil beneath her, as they mixed with him.

Her goodbye burned him. Hours later, the words and thoughts echoed in his mind, unable to be expunged.

Regana felt she had no future now. Jörg understood her point. He had taken her maidenhead in the promise of marrying her. *Not even that at first.* Not until he came to the realization of what he had done. Now many black futures fought to crush her, because of his recklessness.

She could admit the truth to Gawen. For his many faults, her brother doted on Regana. Still, Jörg wasn't sure that even Gawen could protect her from the choosing ceremony. If a Warrior chose her and found her less than intact— He shuddered to consider the many possibilities.

Even if no one chose her, and Jörg couldn't imagine that happening, she would face the difficult task—perhaps impossible task of marrying at all without censure for her state of fall. A life with no man and no children was not one he would wish for Regana. As much as it would kill Jörg to see her in another man's bed, better that than alone, childless, beaten, or dead.

One thing he realized immediately was that he owed her an explanation. Jörg couldn't tell her the whole truth. That much was certain. Knowing the others had used her against him would crush her. Whatever lie he told her depended on one key element. Regana could never think it was her fault. He could never let there be a seed of doubt on that point. Now, after hours of thought, he believed he had the perfect story to ease her mind. She would know that he felt he had no choice but not that the entire plan had hinged on her.

He hid himself, what the Stone called 'ghosting.' Jörg couldn't take the chance of Gawen sensing him before he had a chance to talk to Regana. He had to speak to her alone. Perhaps, after he had convinced her, he could convince Gawen to make a pact with him. He had to put her at ease somehow.

The sight of Gawen sitting up awake shook him. He hadn't counted on that. It was more than halfway through the night. He had planned for Gawen to be lost in sleep in his bed, not vigilant.

Worse, the older man had such a sad look on his face that Jörg started. He shouldn't feel for his former friend. Jörg had been promised no kinder emotions. Still, he could almost swear he felt something resembling compassion for his former brother. It shouldn't be possible, and so he dismissed it. The gods could not be so cruel. Gifted as he was, damned as he was, they could not damn Jörg further with kind emotions he had no hopes of acting on.

One look at Regana made him curse the gods who'd damned him so completely. He still felt for her. Jörg felt not only the longing and pain but also the love. She looked so beautiful in sleep that his mind flashed onto a hundred memories of her smile. He wanted to see her smile, to be the one to make her smile again.

Jörg sat lightly on the edge of her bed and reached to run his hand along her cheek. The blast that pushed him away was painful, and his mind supplied the answer for him automatically. His gaze locked on the amulet that lay over her breast as she scrambled to the wall, shocked awake by the reaction. Regana held the cover to her chest like a shield, and her eyes were wide and frightened.

He ached at the fear in her eyes. "Regana, please," he whispered. "I won't hurt you."

Jörg startled as the door swung open. He had been so shocked, he had forgotten to ghost. Or, was it her amulet that summoned Gawen? He dematerialized as the Warrior shot through the door with his weapons drawn.

Gawen moved to shield his sister, and his *Blutjagd* was a blue fire that surrounded them both. "I know you're still here," he spat. "Show yourself or go."

Jörg streamed out into the night and then he ghosted and came back.

Believing his foe departed, Gawen sheathed his weapons and ran a gentle hand over Regana's tear-streaked cheeks. "Are you all right?" he crooned to her.

Regana wrapped her arms around her waist and her shift strained against her chest in a way that reminded Jörg of their stolen moments together. She nodded mutely.

"Did he touch you?" Gawen's voice was gruff in barely controlled bloodlust.

Jörg felt anger at his assumption that he would—

He realized how truly damned he was. He had done precisely what Gawen accused him of before he touched the Stone.

"Did he?" he demanded.

"My cheek. He touched only my cheek," she replied in a small, broken voice.

Gawen groaned and sank to the bed. He gathered her to his chest gently and held her while she cried. "It's all right, little one," he soothed her, as Jörg had seen him do so many times before. "Veriel is gone from here."

Jörg started. The Stone hadn't named him that. The Stone had not named him at all. How dare they brand him with the name of the Mad Deceiver?

He looked at Regana's broken state and streamed away miserably, his anger forgotten. Perhaps, the one who'd named him wasn't so wrong after all. Veriel, the Destroyer of Lives...

Chapter Three

Pauwel took to his feet as Gawen stormed into the training area. The older man was furious. Whatever was wrong could not be a small thing. The other Warriors sensed it, too. They gathered around him as Gawen faced Sibold.

"We must hunt the beasts," Gawen demanded. "It cannot wait any longer."

"Gawen, Marclef is correct. Between the upcoming battle and the training required, we cannot undertake it at this time. We must wait."

"Then I hunt them myself," he roared.

"What has happened? What has made you lust for their blood?" Sibold asked.

"Veriel—" He took a deep breath and shook his head before continuing in a cold voice. "The beast Veriel came for Regana last night."

"What?" Pauwel thundered. His heartbeat had taken on an alarming cadence.

His brother Warriors covered his explosion with demands for information of their own.

Pauwel barely heard Gawen's answers to them. "She is shaken, but she is fine. No, her amulet protected her. He touched her cheek."

The next few comments went largely unnoticed. Pauwel found himself ordering the information unconsciously. The beast had swept on her while she'd slept. He'd touched her, but her amulet drove him back. He'd fled rather than face Gawen's wrath.

The image of her that came unbidden at Schwertträger's description shook Pauwel to his soul. Regana huddled in her bed weeping was his undoing.

"I stand with you, Gawen," he decided. "We will hunt together. If he haunts your land, I will bring Kethe there, so she will not be unprotected in my home while we hunt."

Gawen looked at him in surprise and nodded slowly. "Thank you, Pauwel."

"I can do no less. You and yours are under attack. I am at your service in this matter."

"No one will hunt them," Sibold decreed. "Gather to protect what is yours, but no one is to seek out confrontation until after the battle. That is my order."

"It is my duty to protect her. You taught me that yourself," Gawen argued.

"I did not order you to hunt. Guard her only."

Pauwel closed his eyes, pushing back the need to avenge his chosen mate. "Then I will help you protect all that is yours," he amended. *Regana. I will help you protect Regana. Veriel will never touch her again,* he vowed.

* * * *

They stood watch for Veriel together for the next three nights, but the beast never showed his face. Gawen watched Pauwel. The young Warrior seemed to get more anxious and angry as the days wore on. Sibold finally collared him while he was pacing the edge of the training area. Gawen moved quickly, knowing the younger man's concerns well.

"Explain yourself," Sibold demanded as Pauwel trained his gaze on the floor sheepishly. "The battle is upon us, Kreuzträger. I know you do not want to join the beasts, so what is your problem?"

Gawen dropped a hand on the younger man's shoulder. "He is worried about leaving the women unprotected," he assured Sibold.

"They're playing with us," Pauwel muttered. "Who will protect the women while we're off in battle? We cannot leave them unguarded."

"Are you trying to claim that duty?" the master trainer asked archly.

Pauwel looked at him in shock. "No. Of course not. I trained for battle. That is my place."

"You have a suggestion of a Warrior to be left behind then?" he prodded.

Pauwel looked around at his brothers, all training and trying studiously to ignore whatever censure Sibold was delivering. He shook his head slowly. "No, Sibold. We will need every man," he decided.

"I agree," Sibold said in approval.

Pauwel nodded miserably and started away.

Sibold called him back. "I notice that there was one Warrior you didn't look at when you considered it, Pauwel," he said evenly.

Pauwel cast his gaze about in confusion. "There was?"

Sibold nodded grimly. "Yes. You did it again," he assured the young man.

"I don't understand."

"You never met my eyes," Sibold informed him.

Pauwel gaped at him. "This is no duty for you," he protested. "You are the greatest of us. Of course, you go to battle. Looking to you was unnecessary."

"No. I am an old man who has seen more than my share of battle. All of you were chosen for this battle. I've trained you well, and I am proud to say that you are all stronger than I ever hoped for you and than I ever hoped to be myself. I trained you to follow Gawen in battle. Never myself. Did it never occur to you that such a move would be unnecessary unless I had no intention of fighting in this battle?

"I was trained as a solitary protector to the people here. That will be my duty while you do yours. Bring home glory to me, and stop worrying about your women. I will protect them with my life if that is what needs be. That is the duty I was trained for."

"Then they will be well protected," Pauwel assured him with a tight smile.

"Now that it is settled, put your mind and arm into training so that you survive to the choosing ceremony," he ordered gruffly but with a fond smile curling his lips.

Chapter Four

Pauwel sat his mount, watching the other lords commit their protected to Sibold at the training area. The open space was big enough to accommodate them all for as many nights as they required to end it. In addition, the building was designed for defense, with its reinforced walls, window slits, and metal doors unlike any building he had ever seen before. Any enemy, human or beast, would have a hard time breaching it if Sibold set his mind to the task. Finally, the Stone would protect the space as well as any friendly being within that space.

He and Kethe had said their farewells at home. Dropping her lightly to the ground by the doorway and watching her walk away had been a fairly painless thing for him, though Pauwel could see the hurt in her eyes when she glanced back at him from the threshold.

What was painful was watching Gawen part from Regana. Pauwel tried to make it appear as if he wasn't watching any family in particular, moving his gaze from person to person, but his attention returned to his chosen wife often.

Though her chin was raised proudly, Pauwel could see the fear in her dark eyes and the slight hitching of her breathing. It was obvious that her brother saw it, too. His hand brushed over her cheek and down the length of her long, black hair to her shoulder. Gawen murmured something to her before he wrapped Regana in his arms.

Pauwel's blood simmered uncomfortably, aching for the day when he could hold her like that. It seemed all he lived for, even more so since Veriel's attack on her person. He was so intent that he didn't realize most of the other lords had mounted up and joined him.

Then Ger spoke. "What's on your mind, Kreuzträger?"

Pauwel smiled crookedly and raised an eyebrow at Ger. "I'm wondering how long the great Lord Schwertträger is going to make us wait for him," he called in a voice designed to cover the entire open space easily.

Gawen turned suddenly and glared at the younger man, while the other lords laughed at his reaction. He sent Regana inside, then mounted his horse and started toward them, looking decidedly dangerous. "Do you need to taste my blade to remember some respect, Kreuzträger?" he warned.

"No, Gawen. After all, we don't want to be late to the battle." He smiled widely as he prodded his horse on. "Not to mention— Well, I wouldn't want you in less than top form for the enemy," he teased over his shoulder.

Gawen matched his stride, raising an eyebrow at the young Warrior. "I see I will have to teach you who the first chosen was," he warned.

"Only because my mother wasn't of marriageable age, old man," he taunted.

Gawen laughed heartily at that barb. "I will remember to take that comment out of what is left of your hide, Kreuzträger."

"I look forward to it," Pauwel assured him.

* * * *

Gawen tapped Ger on the shoulder and pointed to the encampment below. As always, Gawen was their leader, unpartnered so he could move from team to team where he was needed most.

After the others went to the Stone, fighting partners had to be rearranged. Wil and Olbrecht had always been partnered, but Cunczel and Ditrich—now working together—had originally been paired with Dado and Geldric respectively. Ger had originally been matched with Bertolf, while Tilbrand and Redulf— beast both—had been partnered. Now Ger and Pauwel were a pair.

Gawen had always questioned the pairing of Pauwel and Jörg, but Sibold had claimed that they'd balanced each other. Where Pauwel had a cool grace about his fighting, Jörg was more like the legendary berserkers. Even before he went to the Stone, there had been a bit of the beast in Jörg. He had been their strongest Warrior and the worst cursed, as his choice more than proved.

Dusk was upon them and dark coming on fast. The fighters below were eating and preparing for sleep after a long day of travel. The Warriors, on the other hand, were well rested. After finding the place the Stone had foretold for their battle the evening before, they'd had little to do but sleep, eat, and choose their places for the coming attack.

As the sun set and the weary fighters settled next to their fires, Gawen gave the next signal.

A large attacking force on horseback would have alerted them, but seven men on foot in dark clothing, coming silently from three different directions, were a greater danger to them. The sentries were slain without a sound. The horses were led away from dead guards and handlers without causing alarm. When the assault started, there was pandemonium in the camp.

Gawen took them down, one after the other. Still, they came. Though they carried swords, the Warriors were faster, more skilled, and gripped by a stunning *Blutjagd*. Twice, Gawen saw Pauwel take down an enemy posing the danger of flanking Ger only to dance back to those attacking himself for another volley, smooth and patient as always.

"Gawen," Pauwel warned him.

He threw his head around and took down two of the three sneaking up behind him, but the third fell on him and managed to knock Gawen to the ground. Grappling for the other man's sword and pushing it back without much difficulty, Gawen started as the man above him stiffened and rose away with not one but four blades protruding through his chest. As the enemy fighter was tossed like a sack of roots to die far from Gawen, the Warrior met the killer's eyes.

Veriel smiled. "Good evening, Lord Schwertträger. The other half of your forces have arrived to do battle for you," he reported smartly. He reached his hand down, as if to help Gawen to his feet.

Gawen sliced at his outstretched arm and drove him back.

Veriel's smile disappeared, and his eyes glittered red-tinged silver in the firelight. "We're here to keep our word, Gawen. Use us to kill the enemy or die trying to fight us both. The choice is yours, of course."

For a moment, Gawen couldn't find his voice. He nodded stiffly. "If you're here to fight, go fight," he ordered. "You know what to do."

Veriel's head snapped up, and he disappeared like a tendril of smoke as Pauwel pounced on his previous position.

"Are you all right?" the young lord demanded of Gawen, dragging him back to his feet.

He nodded. "Yes. He didn't touch me."

"Trying to kill off Regana's protector?" he asked acidly as he took down another enemy barreling at them.

Gawen scanned the battle. "They are doing the duty they agreed to. There is Draden." He motioned as he took an enemy's throat without taking his gaze from the center of the battle. "And there is Veriel. He says they are all here to fight as agreed."

"Why?"

Gawen shrugged as he strode into the mass of frightened fighters and started to take them on. "I have no idea, but I have a feeling we're going to find out."

* * * *

Jörg stuck mostly to killing with his blade-like claws, feeling most like the style of fighting that he had trained for. The killing styles of the other beasts sickened him.

Cerran and Lorian were ripping out the throats of the panicked fighters with their fangs.

Carstol preferred using his great strength to break their necks or crush their chests in.

Draden had learned to change his form of a fashion. His face was elongated into the snout of a great hairless wolf, his skin stretched grotesquely over the new shape of his face while he mauled whatever came into range.

Resten, the beast Tilbrand, had come up with the most disturbing way to kill of all. With his vicious nature, he was ripping the hearts from the chests of the enemy fighters and piercing them with his teeth for the blood inside before the men even fell.

Overall, the strategy worked well enough. The beasts were in the center and the Warriors around the outside. That kept a buffer zone between the new enemies who were once brothers, but it afforded another advantage. Fighters attempting to escape the beasts were driven into the Warriors and vice versa. It worked so well that the entire battle—seven Warriors and six beasts facing nearly two hundred men—was over in little more than an hour.

The allies faced each other warily across the sea of dead and dying foes. Having not learned how to clean themselves, the other beasts were bathed in blood, both the enemy's and their own. It stained their faces, necks, and teeth in addition to their clothing and hands. The Warriors looked at them in sick distaste before settling their stares on Jörg. As fresh as if he had just bathed, he was in startling contrast to beast and Warrior alike.

"What now, Veriel?" Gawen called out.

Resten interrupted before Jörg could speak. "We go back together," he asserted as if it were a foregone conclusion.

"Back?" Pauwel demanded.

"We were promised—" Resten began.

"He knows nothing of the false promises," Jörg boomed out, closing on Resten. "Ask them. We've done our duty, but as I warned you, the promises were a lie."

"He wouldn't dare," Carstol exclaimed.

"Of course, he would."

"What promises?" Gawen exploded.

Resten shook his head in disbelief. "We were promised all our rights as Warriors, all our property— As long as we fought as beasts and won, we were promised—" He looked at Jörg hopelessly. "Tell them," he roared.

"He lied," Jörg replied smoothly. "I told you, but you refused to believe me."

"What can we do?" Draden asked.

"To get what you were promised? Nothing, just like I told you. To get revenge?" He smiled a cold, calculating smile. "He is mine alone."

"Who is yours?" Ditrich asked quietly.

"Marclef. His life is forfeit only to me." Jörg glared at Resten. "Only one of the lives I intend to take. Would you care to come with me to prove his deceit to our brothers?"

Resten looked at him uncertainly.

"Tonight is not your night to die," Jörg assured him.

"I suppose I have your word on that," the other beast noted acidly.

"You would do well to remember that I always keep my word," he countered.

Resten nodded. "I want to hear the truth for myself." He looked around. "Is one of your gifts controlling a horse?" he asked hopefully.

Jörg smiled widely and shook his head. He grabbed Resten by the arm roughly and pulled him into his sadistic smile. "Try this," he invited, as he forced Resten to dematerialize in his hands. Resten screamed in shock and fear as Jörg dragged his essence over the countryside. The beast's terror and confusion were even more satisfying than the shock evident on the Warrior's faces.

Resten's terror stemmed only partly from not knowing—not knowing how Jörg was forcing his will on him this way, not knowing how he was accomplishing this feat of flying, and not knowing what the younger man's intentions were.

The rest was even more satisfying. Resten feared dematerializing. Better, he loathed the sensation. Even if he survived longer than Jörg planned for him, Resten would never master flight. His beast still forced the process on him before every dawn, having tired of waiting for the burning to distract Resten before completing its task.

When he forced Resten back into his solid form, the man lunged at him with wild eyes. Jörg dematerialized while Resten barreled through him and reappeared as the madman turned to glare at him. "You cannot touch me unless I wish it," Jörg informed him patiently. "Come with me while I collect Marclef."

"Collect? I thought—"

"Sibold will know why I am doing this. Perhaps, if the Warriors know what you were promised, it will go easier on you."

"You don't believe that," Resten whispered.

"No, I don't," he admitted.

* * * *

71

Gawen turned from the space where the two beasts once stood, as Pauwel tore off for the trees. "Pauwel! What are you doing?" he barked.

The younger man stopped and shot him a look of disbelief. "They are going to the village to exercise their rights. Regana, Kethe, Riberta, Anabilia—" He threw up his hands in frustration, as Gawen's eyes widened in understanding.

"And all those who don't have amulets." *Bavin doesn't have an amulet.* "He's right. We have to go now. We can't waste time—" Gawen broke off as he realized that the beasts had gone to ground to protect themselves, until the Warriors left them to finish off the half-dead of the enemy in a healing feeding frenzy. "We go," he ordered, struggling to catch up with Pauwel as the Warrior sprinted to the trees where their horses were sheltered.

They rode as hard as they dared push their horses. If only they had the time to spare to find the horses they'd driven off before the battle, this wouldn't be necessary, but they didn't. As it was, the Warriors were on the edges of self-control every time they had to slow or stop to keep from losing their mounts. Common sense told them that traveling on foot was not an option, but the idea of driving the horses to death on the chance of reaching the village sooner seemed strangely attractive in their desperation.

It was daybreak before they reached the training area. The foul smell assaulted their senses first, the same smell that had wafted over the battlefield from the injured beasts.

"Beast blood," Gawen noted. He strode toward the doorway in the gray half-light with his weapons up, unsure of how much light was required to send a beast to ground.

"Where is Sibold?" Wil asked him, as Gawen crouched to examine a dark stain on the packed earth.

"Inside. Dragged inside," he assured them after confirming to himself that the track he was examining was human blood and not beast.

Pauwel strode to the doors and pushed one back in annoyance, obviously tired of playing at hiding with the beasts. Too late to stop him, Gawen launched after the headstrong young Warrior. As Pauwel ducked into the darkness beyond the door, Gawen saw the attack coming. He grasped the wrist that held the blade headed for Pauwel firmly as the other man spun away.

Gawen swung one of his own blades for the unseen enemy's throat. The feminine cry of fear stopped him in his tracks. He dragged the woman into the soft light filtering through the doorway, as her cry set off sobs and screams from the far reaches of the pitch black room. Brown eyes met his and widened in surprise. Gawen dropped his blade and dragged her to his chest.

"Regana," he rasped into her hair. Gawen knew he was shaking, but he couldn't seem to help himself. He could have killed her. Without his instruction, Regana dropped the blade in her hand to the floor, and he relaxed his grip on her wrist to wrap his arms around her fully.

"Gawen?" Ger asked, a tentative note in his voice.

"Light the fires. We have to see what we're dealing with." In the meantime, he brushed his hand over her hair and soothed Regana while she shook. "What were you doing?" he finally inquired as the fires were lit.

"I thought they'd found a way in," she managed.

73

His anger resurfaced suddenly. "They would have killed you. Why would you try something like this?" he demanded.

"Sibold gave me his weapons. What else was I to assume I was supposed to do?" she asked weakly.

Gawen was still struggling with the improbability of such a thing when he got a good look at her in the new lights being lit all over the building. Her clothing was stained with blood, and smudges of it marked her face and hands, human blood. Gawen ran his hands over her looking for some sign that he—or anyone had injured her.

Regana shook her head in understanding and half-dragged him toward the shadowed depths of the room. "It's Sibold's blood," she corrected him. "He wants to see you." She hesitated and shuddered. "If..."

Gawen lengthened his stride, passing between the protected family members huddled on the floor. He noted that they sank back in shock, but their eyes weren't locked on him. They seemed wary of Regana for some reason, but he didn't have the time to question that now.

Ditrich was already at Sibold's side when he arrived. He looked up at Gawen and shook his head. "The damage is too severe. There is nothing that can be done."

Gawen nodded and knelt to lay a hand on Sibold's shoulder as Ditrich wandered away in search of his family.

The master trainer opened his eyes and smiled weakly. "Battle is for the young, Gawen."

"You kept them safe. You gave your life to keep them safe, just as you promised."

"Now that is your duty. You know the Stone chose you to be my replacement."

"I could never replace you," Gawen protested weakly.

"You are the Stone's lord. You are the master trainer. You must train them to fight the beasts."

"I only know what little you've taught us so far."

Sibold growled out his displeasure. "You have a duty, and you will perform that duty. The Stone will guide you."

Gawen tightened his jaw and nodded. "I will do my duty," he agreed.

Sibold looked past his shoulder, and Gawen followed his gaze to Regana, standing quietly at the edge of the crowd of protected that distanced themselves from her carefully. "You have another duty," he whispered.

Gawen nodded and met his eyes. "Yes, I know."

"The beasts will not rest in their quest to take her from you now. I gave her my weapons to give her some protection until you came for her."

"Why? Why do they want her?"

"She is different than the other women. She is a fighter. The Stone will explain, when the time is right. For now, just know that they will pursue her." He looked to Regana again. "Call her."

"Regana," Gawen ordered.

She surged forward and knelt across Sibold's body from her brother. Regana took the dying man's hand gently. "Do you need something?" she asked.

Sibold laughed lightly and touched her cheek with one gnarled hand. "For hours, you have asked me that.

What I need is your safety. You do not follow orders well, young woman," he scolded.

Regana darkened and flicked a wary look at Gawen that made his heart pound. She smiled weakly as she met Sibold's eyes again. "So my brother has told me many times, and so you have warned him that I would not almost as many," she admitted.

"It is all right," Sibold soothed her. "I have indeed made that prediction of you many times. I owe my life, living long enough to pass his duty to him properly, to your headstrong nature. I should have known the Stone would protect you."

Regana nodded. "I'd prefer not to make my brother an old man by telling him the tale," she teased.

"You must," Sibold told her. "You must tell Gawen everything. Until he knows the whole tale, he will not know his path."

Regana swallowed hard, then nodded.

Sibold tightened his grip on her hand. His eyes were suddenly piercing. "Everything, Regana. The Stone cannot lead him properly to all he must do until he knows everything you have to tell."

She met Gawen's eyes and nodded. "I understand, Sibold."

But there was something in her eyes that was new, something dark and closed off where Regana had always been open to him before. Gawen knew that she would not willingly tell him everything, whatever everything was.

Sibold lived long enough for the transfer of power, as the Stone requested of him. There was no question when Gawen crossed to the Stone and unsheathed his blades. He crossed them before his face and laid them on the Stone. The surge of power was like a cold wave washing up his arms and gripping his mind in a numbing rush. Before the Stone released him, it passed an amazing amount of information to him.

Talking to the Stone was maddening. At times, it was clear and concise in its instructions—how to kill beasts, their limitations, and so forth. Sometimes, it talked in riddles—strategies and timelines for defeating them. With regard to Regana, the Stone was absolutely still and silent.

Released at last, Gawen sank to his knees and tried to catch his breath, his muscles unknotting. His gaze moved from Warrior to Warrior and settled on Regana. Regana with hidden secrets in her eyes, suddenly feared by the villagers, and a black spot in his seemingly bottomless well of knowledge.

Gawen met Pauwel's eyes, pushing stiffly to his feet. "Send the protected ones home," he instructed. "We have much to discuss."

He grabbed his sister lightly by the arm as she tried to brush past him toward the doors. "Not you. You have a story to tell." She slid her gaze from his and headed back into the room.

* * * *

Regana sat with her back to the wall, watching the Warriors nervously. Everything? There was no way she could tell them everything. She looked at the Stone and bit her lip in worry. Would the Stone tell Gawen if she lied? Worse, would it really refuse to lead him if she did? Regana shuddered at the thought.

She started as she realized that Gawen was watching her intently. His eyes were narrowed in a way that made her blood run cold, and she tightened her jaw stubbornly in response. He nodded in challenge as he stalked toward her, looking every bit the Warrior and not at all the brother she loved. Regana supposed that made what she had to do easier.

The other lords dropped to the ground in a semi-circle around her, but Gawen stood with his arms crossed over his broad chest and his eyes cold and hard. "What happened last night?" he asked. "We've heard a lot of unbelievable stories. We need the truth."

Regana nodded. This much, she could tell him. "I woke when Sibold started putting out the torches."

"Why?"

"He said he didn't want the beasts to see inside easily. I helped him put out all the fires and get the protected against the far wall. Then he went outside."

"But not you?"

She felt her cheeks darken. "Of course, he told me to stay with the others," she admitted.

"Why didn't you?"

Regana shrugged hopelessly and let her breath out in a huff. "I don't know. I just went."

"Outside?" Pauwel demanded.

She shook her head and pointed to the window slits by the door. "Just there to see what was happening."

"What did happen?" Wil asked.

"Sibold was out on the path. I could see three men approach."

"Three?" Olbrecht asked in confusion.

"Marclef," Pauwel surmised.

"And two beasts with him," she supplied.

"Resten and Veriel," Gawen corrected her.

She looked at him in confusion.

"Tilbrand and Jörg?" His patience was obviously straining.

His attitude annoyed her as much as the sick sensation in the pit of her stomach did. "If you already know everything, why are you bothering to ask?" she snapped back at him.

"I don't know everything," he noted, a touch of sarcasm biting at his words.

"Of course." Regana took a deep breath and began again. "Jörg...Veriel," she managed weakly, "insisted Marclef tell Sibold the truth about the beasts." She furrowed her brow. "He kept saying 'the others,' as if he wasn't..." She struggled to find the words to express the separateness he was expressing.

Gawen nodded. "Did Marclef admit to promising them their rights?"

Regana glared at him. "I thought you didn't know this story?"

Her brother tightened his jaw dangerously.

"Yes, he admitted it. He begged Sibold to accept it, but Sibold explained why it wasn't possible."

"What happened next?" Cunczel interjected.

"Resten went mad. He started demanding his rights. He grabbed Marclef by the throat and demanded that he find a way to keep his word." She shuddered at the memory.

"Did they kill Marclef?" Ditrich asked.

"I don't know."

They looked at her expectantly.

"Veriel removed Resten's hands and took Marclef from him. He told Resten to go tell his brothers they had been lied to while he took care of Marclef's treachery." Regana considered the chill that had passed through her when Jörg seemed to meet her eyes directly in the darkness and shuddered again. "Somehow, that seemed worse," she admitted. "He took Marclef away into the trees, east. I don't know where."

"What about Resten?" Ger asked suddenly. "Did he go with them?"

"No, he didn't. When the others were gone, he demanded his rights of Sibold. He demanded to choose his mate."

"Why didn't he take a woman from the village? An unprotected one?" Wil asked.

"He said his chosen mate was in here," she answered simply.

"Did he say who?" Gawen demanded.

Regana looked at him in surprise. His face was set in harsh, angry lines and his eyes were emotionless as a snake's. Gawen was abruptly someone that she didn't recognize at all.

She shook her head and pressed her back into the wall. "No. He just said that she was inside."

He nodded stiffly. "Resten tried to force his way in?"

She nodded. "Sibold held him off as long as he could. He even wounded him. You saw what Resten did in return." Regana swallowed a sour lump at the memory of the pain the beast had inflicted on the master trainer. "Once Sibold had been defeated, Resten charged at the doors, but he was thrown back when he touched them."

"So, he couldn't get in," Ditrich prodded.

"He grabbed Sibold and demanded to know the secret of how to get inside. When he found out that the Stone would never let him pass the doors, he ordered Sibold to bring us out or lose his life. Sibold refused."

"What happened?" Olbrecht asked.

"Veriel appeared out of nowhere, and they started fighting. He had some sort of weapon with a lot of blades on it."

"Did you see this weapon?" Gawen asked.

"It was too dark to see it clearly. I thought he was going to kill Resten, but he stopped. I could hear them arguing. For some reason, he couldn't kill him." She shrugged. "I can't explain it any better than that."

Gawen nodded. "The beast elders can only be killed by a Warrior. They can't kill each other."

"What did he do?" Ger asked.

"I don't know."

They all stared at her intently, and she groaned in frustration.

"Am I to blame if Veriel kept dragging his—prey, victims, whatever they are—out of my field of vision? All I can tell you is that they left."

"Not by Resten's choice, obviously," Wil noted.

"Then what?" Gawen asked.

Regana grimaced. "They were gone, and Sibold was hurt." Her brother glared at her, and she winced at the coming scene.

"You went out there?" Pauwel exploded.

"Have you gone mad?" Ditrich asked.

"You had the Stone to protect you in here," Olbrecht noted.

"Sibold was here to protect you, not the other way around," Wil shot at her.

"Let her tell the story," Gawen demanded over the riot of other voices.

She sighed. "I tried to get the others to help, but no one would. The most help I could get was help with the doors if—when I made it back in."

"So you walked right out and brought Sibold in?" Gawen snapped.

"Don't make it sound so easy. Yes, I went out there, and yes, I dragged him back to the doors." She hesitated.

"And?" Gawen prodded.

"And...Veriel came back before I was back inside," she admitted sheepishly. Surely, the others had already told him that much, so it shouldn't be new information for him. "We were so close. I couldn't leave Sibold a mere body length from the doors. So, I pulled harder and made it all the way to the doorway, but the others wouldn't let us in because they could see Veriel." Regana grimaced at the memory of the argument behind the doors that had ended in the decision to keep them closed. "Veriel—said he wanted to help."

"Help? Help how?" Gawen asked.

"I don't know, and I wasn't prepared to find out. So..." She met his eyes and grimaced again. "I pulled Sibold's blade from his hand and threatened Veriel with it."

"What did he think of that?"

"I am sure he wasn't very happy about it, but he backed off."

"He backed off but he didn't leave," Gawen noted.

Regana shook her head.

"What did he say?"

She sighed. "He was trying to convince me to put the weapon down."

Gawen raised an eyebrow in disbelief.

"He tried to convince me that he didn't pose a danger to us, and he claimed that he hadn't chosen his course—to become beast, I mean."

"How did you respond to that?"

"How do you think, Gawen? I had just seen him drag a man and a beast away, and neither of them came back."

He stared at her intently.

"All right. I told him I'd plant the blade between his eyes if he didn't leave."

Gawen rubbed his forehead roughly. "What did he say to that courteous offer?"

"He—" She furrowed her brow.

"Regana?"

"It was rather disconcerting," she admitted. "It was...like talking to Jörg. Just Jörg."

He stared, confused.

"The same jokes, the same looks. He still treats me like I'm seven. He always treated me like that. I can't explain it," she decided in frustration.

"He was trying to lull you into trusting him," Gawen decided. "Did he say why?"

"No, but it didn't work."

"Good thing," he mused.

"I wouldn't have come back either," she decided miserably.

"Most likely not." Gawen stared at the Stone. "What else?"

"When he realized I wasn't going to drop my guard, he left."

"You mean he disappeared."

"No, he walked away into the trees," she insisted.

"Why?"

Regana hesitated. "I don't know. Maybe, so the others would see he was gone? Maybe, so they'd let us back in? I don't know. He didn't exactly explain himself."

Gawen was quiet for a long moment. "What else?" he prodded.

"They let us in. Kethe, Anabilia, and I tried to stop Sibold's bleeding. I tried to give his weapon back, but he told me to keep it, then handed me the other as well."

"Why?"

"For protection."

"Whose protection?"

"Everyone, I suppose."

"Why you? Why not one of the men?"

Regana groaned and buried her face in her hands. "I don't know. Maybe because I was willing to use it against Veriel. Maybe because I was the only one who came out to get him. You should have asked Sibold while you had the chance."

"Didn't you?" he demanded.

"No, I guess I never really thought about it," she admitted. "I had other, more pressing, problems on my mind, like trying to keep Sibold alive."

Gawen seemed to consider that. "What else?"

"You know the rest. We waited for daybreak. We'd planned to send someone for Landric when the sun was up. That was when you arrived. I didn't know who you were, because you didn't announce yourselves, and I didn't want to chance the beasts seeing me at the window slit, so I attacked the first person through the door."

"What else?" he demanded.

Regana rubbed her head. She was really starting to loathe that refrain. "I don't know what else you want. That's it. That's all that happened last night."

"What else did Veriel say?"

She stared, exhaustion weighing her down. "I'm tired, Gawen. He just kept trying to convince me that he wanted to help and that he wasn't a danger—over and over."

"There has to be something else," he insisted.

"There were people just behind the doors. There were people at the window slits. Ask them. For the love of all that's holy, I don't remember anything else."

Gawen ran his hand over the beard on his chin and regarded her with a look that chilled her. "Come with me," he ordered.

A few of the other lords started to rise.

"Alone," he qualified.

Regana followed him outside, trying to ignore the looks on the other men's faces. She wasn't sure what the Stone was telling him, but she knew it wasn't good. Gawen motioned for her to sit at the base of a tree and sat facing her.

"Regana, I need to know what you're not telling me. It's just me now. If Sibold felt you knew something important, you do."

"Then, he should have told me what it was," she commented miserably.

"What exactly did Veriel say?"

"When I threatened to use the weapon, he teased me about how I could never win a fight with him. He always teased me about that, how I had to pout to win against him. He reminded me of times we got into trouble together as children. He talked about regrets. I really don't understand what was so important, Gawen."

"There are two possibilities. Either you really have no idea what I need to know, or you're lying to me." He met her eyes, and she had to steel herself not to look away. "I know you're hiding something from me. I can see it in your eyes. I can see it in the way you avoid my eyes. There is nothing you cannot tell me."

"There is nothing to tell."

"There is, and until you confide in me, the Stone cannot help me protect you. It will not help me. Do you understand?"

Regana sighed and planted her chin on her knees. She was spent. What difference would telling Gawen really make? Then again, why would the whole story be of any importance to anyone but herself? She yawned and tried to fight her eyes open.

"Why are you lying to me?" Gawen asked quietly.

"I've told you everything you wanted to know. I've told you the truth, Gawen," she managed sleepily.

"Go home," he ordered. "Take my horse."

She pushed to her feet and headed for his mount.

Gawen lifted her into the saddle gently. He took the reins from her and patted the horse's shoulder. "You'll have to tell me soon, Regana," he whispered.

Her heart started to pound, and she was suddenly wide-awake. "What do you mean?" she asked evenly, though she was terrified. Her mind shut down at the possible things he might be referring to. Regana couldn't think about that. She wouldn't consider all the consequences of her actions, here and now, with Gawen watching her.

"If Sibold is right, things are only going to get worse until you tell me. How bad will you let it get before you trust me?"

"I do trust you, Gawen," she assured him.

Gawen was probably the only one she could trust now, but Regana couldn't expect him to protect her against the rest of the world. If the others knew that she had been going to Jörg's bed for all that time, they would only see her lying with a beast. Nothing could be gained by that.

* * * *

Gawen uttered a number of colorful curses as he made his way back inside. The other men looked at him uneasily.

"Did she say anything?" Wil asked.

"Nothing that helped me understand. If only the Stone would tell me what I'm looking for," he commented in frustration.

"Sibold gave you no clue?" Ditrich asked.

"None. He seemed to think Regana would know what to tell me, and I'd recognize it immediately."

"Could she be lying to you?" Ger asked.

Gawen hesitated. He knew she was, but he wasn't about to tell the others that and risk one of them confronting her about it. This was between Regana and himself. "She could, but I don't know why she would," he admitted.

"What do we do?" Pauwel asked solemnly.

"Nothing. I'll keep prodding her for information. In the meantime, we have more important things to do."

"For instance?" Will asked.

"I need to teach you all the Stone has shown me about killing beasts."

* * * *

It was after nightfall when they finally broke from training and headed to their homes. By the time Gawen reached the other side of the village, only Pauwel and Ditrich were still with him, preparing to take the paths to their own homes.

Gawen drew his weapon before the two beasts materialized, and the other two Warriors moved just after him.

Veriel threw the other beast at their feet and smiled. "I could kill this beast," he informed them. "I choose to let you do the honors. I want him to understand what he has inflicted on others."

The beast on the ground pushed to his feet in a series of jerky movements that seemed forced. His skin was gray, and he was obviously weakened for them and in need of feeding. He met their eyes miserably.

"Marclef," Ditrich breathed as he reached toward the leader reflexively.

Gawen grabbed his hand and pushed it back. "No. He is not human. He has been turned."

"Beg them, Marclef," Veriel taunted him. "See if they will spare your life now that you are no better than the other beasts you helped create."

"I didn't want this," Marclef moaned.

"Did I?" the beast elder countered. "As I recall, you gave me ample reason, but did I want this?"

"I know your secrets, Jörg. I—" He stopped speaking and started gasping for breath. His fingers clawed at his throat hopelessly as if trying to pull off fingers invisible to the eye.

"My secrets are not yours to tell," he chided Marclef. "The death I would give you would be infinitely more painful than any death the Warriors will grant you. I could happily torture you for days before I kill you. I could force you to feed, so you will know what monsters you created. I am being generous by granting you a quick death and kind executioners, Marclef. I warned you at the Stone that no one would save you from me. Do not forget that promise, and do not forget your place."

Marclef sucked in a deep breath as the elder released his hold on him. "How?" he croaked.

"I turned you. That means I retain leading strings on you. I can see all you do or think to do. I control what I permit you to do, even from a distance. My secrets are my own."

Marclef nodded and surged forward as if he had been pushed. "Kill me," he requested of them. "For the love of all that's holy, kill me."

"Why?" Pauwel asked. "Why should we do Veriel any favors?"

The elder shrugged. "You will be kind in killing him. I will not. It is Marclef you are showing mercy to. I would not balk at killing him myself, as slowly and painfully as I can." His smile widened at the thought.

Gawen took Marclef's heart without taking his gaze from Veriel. "There! Your puppet is destroyed and your amusement along with it. What secret did he know?" he asked.

"You'll never know, not from one of my puppets and not from me," he taunted.

"What do you want with Regana?"

Veriel's eyes narrowed and his smile dimmed somewhat. "She amuses me. No human man would dare threaten to plant a blade in me. She has spirit that I find refreshing."

"Stay away from her, Veriel," he warned.

The beast laughed. "A threat, Gawen? Perhaps the spirit is simply a family trait."

"I don't care what it is. Regana doesn't want your attention. Look elsewhere for your next meal."

His smile disappeared. "I would never feed on Regana," he growled.

"But you would—what? Amuse yourself with her?" he accused.

"Perhaps not, Gawen. Perhaps, it is too late for games." Veriel dematerialized and streamed away.

Gawen sheathed his weapons and stormed toward his home with Pauwel at his heels. He vaguely registered that Ditrich had turned back to town, presumably to notify Marclef's brothers to dispose of him properly.

"Where are you going, Pauwel?" he growled.

"What are you doing?" the younger man countered.

"Getting answers," he snapped.

"Then I am making sure you don't kill her," he commented evenly.

"This isn't a joke, Pauwel."

"I didn't say it was. I'm serious."

Gawen stopped and stared at him in shock. "You think I'd hurt her?"

"I've never seen you so cold for a kill. I've never seen you this angry. Honestly, I don't know what you're capable of right now."

He nodded uncertainly. "Come on. You may be right," he conceded. In truth, Gawen had visions of shaking the truth from her, and that was not a sane response. He started walking again, confusion slowing his step a bit.

Pauwel matched his pace. "Why do you think he wants Regana to trust him?" he asked.

"They pursue her."

"You think Resten wanted her when he demanded his mate?"

"I know it. Sibold told me as much."

"Why Regana?"

"I don't know. She's different than other women."

"Her coloring, you mean?"

"More than that. Veriel mentioned her spirit. Sibold talked about her being a fighter. It has something to do with that, but I don't know what."

"What does the Stone say?"

"It doesn't."

Pauwel snapped a startled look at him.

"The Stone doesn't tell me anything about Regana. It won't."

Pauwel nodded uncertainly, but he didn't ask whatever was on his mind.

At the house, Regana looked at them warily. "You're late," she commented.

"We had something to take care of," Gawen replied evasively.

"Dinner, Pauwel?" she offered.

"No. Kethe will have something for me. Thank you."

"It's no trouble," she assured him. She moved to the fire and started to fill the bowl she had waiting for Gawen.

"Regana, what was Jörg's secret?" her brother asked suddenly, trying to take her off guard.

She stilled for a moment before turning and placing the bowl on the table. "What secret? All the secrets I know are years old. I hardly think sneaking out with his father's bow when he was nine to hunt wolves was the secret you had in mind."

"He snuck out to hunt wolves when he was nine?" Pauwel asked in amusement. "How would you know?"

Gawen sighed. "Jörg told her everything." His eyes narrowed as Regana darkened. "Regana?"

"I went with him," she admitted.

Gawen felt his blood burn. "Sit! Now."

Regana raised an eyebrow.

"Yes, I'm ordering you, and if you know what is good for you, you will do as I say this time. Sit."

She took her seat and sighed. "Yes, Gawen?"

"How could you possibly—" He stopped in frustration, trying to get a handle on his anger.

"Sneak out? You are quite a heavy sleeper," Regana replied coyly.

"Risk yourself like that," he qualified.

"I was eight. You were hunting then."

"Not wolves," Gawen protested.

"Children do stupid things. They don't realize what the consequences of their actions are." She seemed far away for a moment.

Gawen shook his head. "You changed the subject on purpose, didn't you?"

"I was making a point, Gawen. I don't know what use anything I know could be. Who cares what he did when he was eight or ten? You need to know about the last week. That is information I cannot provide."

"What about the last year?"

She shook her head slowly. "You saw him as often as I did. What could I know that you don't?" she reasoned.

Gawen watched as she rubbed her scar nervously, the thin line of some blood oath she had taken with Jörg when they were children. That oath represented just one in a whole line of things she hadn't told him where Jörg was concerned—and still wouldn't. Gawen had tried several times in the last week. Regana simply answered that one could not have an oath with a being that had no honor.

He grumbled dangerously. "Jörg had a secret he'd rather kill Marclef than have me know. If you know that secret, you have to tell me."

Regana paled considerably. "He did kill Marclef," she breathed.

"Are you all right?" Pauwel asked, no doubt trying to get Gawen to back down somewhat.

"I don't feel well," she admitted.

"Regana, this is getting us nowhere," Gawen barked.

"I don't know what secret Marclef knew," she whispered. "I hope I never do." Regana met his eyes miserably and headed for her bedchamber at a run.

Pauwel watched her go in confusion. "What do you think? Is she lying?" he asked quietly.

"Absolutely, but she's lying for a reason. She's terrified of something. I just wish I knew what."

Chapter Five

Gawen grumbled to himself as he pulled his best tunic over his freshly bathed body. Regana had made it for him months ago for this night, and though he knew that the trim covered a few minor errors in construction, it had been lovingly made for him by her, and he would not point out the faults in craftsmanship for anything.

This was supposed to be a happy night, but all he could think of were problems. Part of it was the delay in the choosing ceremony. All the Warriors were on edge, but until Thorald had been chosen and accepted as village leader, there could be no ceremony.

Gawen made sure he was included in the choice of the new leader, citing Marclef's deception to secure a strong voice in the appointment. Thorald had been the youngest man considered by far, but he was strong in his convictions and would not betray his people or their protectors.

The whole mess cost them two weeks of time that the Warriors should have been allowed to actively print on their mates. They were little better than snarling beasts now.

Regana still refused to take part in the choosing. She claimed that she had no wish to marry a Warrior. That, in itself, bothered him. If beasts pursued her, being wed to a Warrior was the safest place for her. Of course, Gawen already protected her, and he was in no hurry to relinquish his duty to someone else, though some days she tried his patience until he felt he might go mad.

Regana still wouldn't tell him why she'd changed her mind, though he knew in his heart that Veriel was to blame somehow.

She also refused to tell him whatever secret she was hiding from him. More than once in the two weeks, Gawen had stormed away to keep from doing her physical harm.

He had tried every approach conceivable, and she had steadfastly refused to be drawn into the discussion. No amount of force worked. Putting her at ease failed, though Regana seemed less at ease in general than Gawen had ever seen her. Reassurances swayed her only momentarily, but never enough to get her to confide in him. He worried about her safety— and his own sanity if she didn't tell him soon.

Gawen strapped on his weapons belt and looped the amulet for Bavin around the hilt of one of his weapons securely. His printing had been gnawing at him so intently that he'd actually spoken to Bavin to reassure himself that she had not removed herself from the choosing. He had been gladdened by her surprise and her rather shy confirmation.

He had discovered soon that the move had created its own set of problems. The stolen looks Bavin had cast him ever since had him aching for her. He had argued with himself that the battle was over and his right to choose was guaranteed, but Gawen ultimately decided that he would not do Bavin the dishonor of taking her before the ceremony. He smiled at the knowledge that he could kiss her at the ceremony and take her to mate as soon as she was willing. He prayed that she would be willing soon.

His smile faltered somewhat at the sight of Regana staring into the flames. She had been so volatile and unpredictable lately that Gawen felt he was living with a stranger. At times, he expected her to argue with him, and she would stare at him sadly or stop speaking to him entirely. At times, he expected her to laugh and smile for him, and she got angry and stormed off or looked at him warily as if she expected some trap from him. Gawen sighed as he realized Regana had not smiled an honest, joyful smile since at least the night Marclef died, probably earlier than that.

"It's time, Regana. Are you ready?" he asked.

She didn't look away from the fire. "I'm not going."

"Of course, you're going. The entire village is going."

"Everyone but me. I'm not participating, Gawen. There is no point in going."

"Come to see me choose then," he invited, forcing his tone lighter.

Regana shook her head. "I'd rather not."

Gawen sighed in frustration. "I cannot protect you, if you are nowhere near me," he challenged.

"Your amulet protects me. Your training blades are in your chest. That's worked in the past," she commented ruefully.

"I can't leave you unprotected," he decided.

"You can't leave Bavin waiting for you at the ceremony. Go choose her. I'll be fine."

Gawen looked at her in shock. "How did you know my choice?" he asked.

Regana smiled a sad, secretive smile. "I know most of the chosen. Ditrich is choosing Anabilia. Ger is choosing Ingela. Wil is choosing Evfemia. Olbrecht is

97

torn between Ingela and Lenne, so he will choose Lenne after Ger makes his choice. Cunczel is undecided, but I believe he will choose Lela since Riberta annoys him and Giana is too quiet even for him."

"What about Pauwel and Kethe?" he asked archly.

"None of the Warriors favor Kethe that I know of. I know Cunczel thinks she's too outspoken. She has another admirer who hopes she is not chosen tonight. I don't know who Pauwel favors," she admitted.

"How could you know all of this?"

"It's not difficult when you watch closely enough. Go on, Gawen. Don't be late to your own choosing."

He hesitated. "Did anyone favor you?"

She shrugged. "No one who is left does, so what does it matter? Obviously, those who went to the Stone didn't have anything to lose, so I suppose not."

"What about Pauwel? You don't know who he favors. You admitted that."

She met his eyes again uncertainly, then shook her head. "He doesn't want me," she decided. "He wants someone, but it's not me."

"How can you be so sure?"

"I'm sure. Go Gawen. You're late." She motioned him toward the door.

Gawen nodded in confusion and went. His mind kept turning the conversation over and over while he walked, but he only created more questions. If Gawen had watched closely enough, would he have the key to unlocking Regana's problem?

* * * *

The Warriors followed Gawen into the training area. Nine women stood across from them. As if by some unspoken agreement, the men who had already latched onto a particular woman were permitted to move to the front of the line.

Gawen thought it impossible, but he found himself distracted from the thought of claiming Bavin. He found himself drawn to Pauwel's expression as Kreuzträger scanned the women who waited for choosing. He kept his expression studiously even, but he never once stopped on a face. When he was done, he nodded and walked to the rear of the line. Gawen's heart sank. Whatever woman Pauwel had been counting on was not present, but before he could corner the young Warrior, the ceremony started.

"Gawen, Lord Schwertträger, Stone lord and master trainer," Thorald boomed out. "Stand forth now and choose your wife and mate."

Gawen crossed the room to the women and took Bavin's hands gently. "I choose Bavin, if she will have me."

Bavin smiled and blushed deeply.

"Does any man protest this match?" Thorald asked.

Silence greeted him for a reply, and Gawen felt his muscles relax.

"How deep is your need, Gawen? Is the joining ceremony one moon hence sufficient to you?"

Knowing that he could pursue Bavin and take her if she was willing charged him. He could wait for a formal ceremony forever if need be. "I am content with waiting, Thorald."

The other Warriors were called forth one by one and chose their mates with no interference from another. Predictably, all announced that they were content to wait for the joining to take their chosen wives into their homes. By the sixth, they stood hand in hand with their mates: Gawen with Bavin, Ditrich with Anabilia, Cunczel with Lela, Ger with Ingela, Wil with Evfemia, and Olbrecht with Lenne. Regana had been right on every match.

Finally, only Pauwel remained for the Warriors. Giana, Riberta, and Kethe remained for the women. Kethe smiled at her brother and left the floor.

"Pauwel Lord Kreuzträger, stand forth and choose your wife and mate," Thorald called.

Pauwel crossed halfway to the two women and stopped. Giana looked distinctly nervous. Riberta was smug almost to the point of appearing predatory. Pauwel moved his gaze back and forth between them, and a muscle tightened in his jaw.

"I choose..." He looked from one to the other again and closed his eyes. He shook his head and met Thorald's eyes resolutely. "I choose not to marry at this time," he decided.

The assembled villagers roared in distress, and Thorald held up a hand to still them. "Pauwel, these women have agreed to marry. Your curse demands—"

"Do not tell me what the curse demands. I know what it demands. At this time, it does not demand me to choose a mate. I will not choose until it makes that demand of me. As for the women, they may consider themselves free of their obligation to me this night."

"And when the time comes, if the woman is unwilling?" the leader demanded.

"Then I die at Gawen's blade," he answered simply, in a quiet, disinterested voice that frightened the master trainer.

"You are determined?" Thorald asked.

"I am. I will not choose at this time."

"Very well. As it is your right to choose a mate, it is your right not to choose."

Pauwel nodded and returned to the doorway.

Giana left the floor, her face a mask of relief. Riberta glared at the young Warrior before she stormed away. Gawen shuddered at Pauwel's choices: Giana, who doubtless agreed out of a sense of duty, or Riberta. It would have surprised Gawen if any Warrior had chosen the self-centered beast that had the face of an angel.

"You have chosen your women. Protect them, now," Thorald decreed.

Six amulets appeared in unison. Six men placed them lovingly around the necks of their chosen women, gave their blessings, and sealed the match. Some sealed it passionately, some in a chaste exchange. The one who worried Gawen was the one who sealed no one to himself that night.

Bavin stared up at him, blushing demurely, and Gawen cursed himself for allowing anything to steal his attention from her.

"Go, Gawen. You are master trainer, and you must see to him. I will be waiting for you when you are free to come to me," she finished shyly.

Gawen kissed her passionately. "I will come for you very soon," he promised her. He squeezed her hand and launched across the open area after Pauwel, dodging well-wishers on the way. It took him only a few minutes to catch up to Pauwel as he walked from the festivities, looking angry and dangerous.

"Pauwel, hold," he demanded.

The young Warrior sighed and stopped.

"Why?" he asked simply.

"I could not bind myself to either of them. I could not do it," he replied, his face all harsh lines in the gathering darkness.

"I can't blame you," Gawen joked lightly.

Pauwel smiled a tight smile at that.

"Walk with me," he invited.

Kreuzträger's smile disappeared, and he nodded sadly as he started moving again.

"Who is she, Pauwel? Who has captured you so that no other woman will find your heart open?"

He looked away. "Someone who does not care for me. That much is obvious. Without a kind eye from her, it is all meaningless."

"Are you sure no other will do?"

"I'm not certain of anything but that Riberta and Giana will not."

Gawen nodded in relief. "Have you spoken to the lady?" he asked.

"Of course not," Pauwel snapped. "It would not have been appropriate to announce my intentions. It would not have been kind. What if I had approached her and then died in battle? I could not live with hurting her that way."

"Have you thought of speaking to her at this point? Perhaps, she might consent to marry if she knew your feelings. Perhaps, it was only the crush of the ceremony that frightened her and she would look favorably upon you personally."

He seemed uncertain for the first time. "What if she doesn't look favorably on me? If she rebuffs me, I die."

"You die if you let this continue. Think about it."

Pauwel nodded miserably. "I should go back for Kethe. Night is falling."

"She will want to stay and celebrate with friends. The others will see her home. I know Ditrich and Ger will. Come home with me for a quiet meal and a drink."

Pauwel shook his head miserably. "I'd rather be alone, Gawen."

"Then as master trainer, I order you. This is not a good time for you to be alone."

The young Warrior smiled tightly again. "For my own good?" he guessed.

"Certainly."

"Don't you have a chosen to be a nuisance to?" Pauwel complained.

"She bade me tend to you. If I do less, I bring her displeasure down on myself," he theorized.

"Well then...I suppose I have no choice in the matter."

They walked in silence, drinking in the cool, night air as the moon rose over the trees.

Gawen swept the door to his home open happily. "Regana, we have a guest," he announced. When she didn't appear from one of the rooms, he furrowed his brow. "Regana?"

He moved from room to room, glancing into the bedchambers and pantry in increasing apprehension. The fire was banked and blazing. If Regana left, it was not long ago.

"Gawen? Could she have gone to the ceremony late?" Pauwel inquired.

"No. We would have passed her on the road."

"Then where—"

He got no further. Regana's voice, high in panic, reached them. "No," she screamed. "You can't do it."

Pauwel launched through the open door toward the sound of her voice with Gawen close behind. Their weapons were drawn even before they shot up the path into the trees.

* * * *

Regana paced the floor. Her emotions were a knot within her. She had snapped at Gawen when he'd appealed to her to come to the choosing. Even if she were not to participate, she could still have watched him choose. He'd left in an obvious upset at her stubborn refusal.

She couldn't go. It was that simple. It wasn't just her own lost aspirations of being chosen by Jörg. If it was just that, she could probably have managed to make the requested appearance and nursed her hurt. Regana wouldn't be chosen, now or ever. She had surrendered her maidenhead, and allowing another man access to her would generate too many questions that she could not bear to answer—or that might cost her her life in the answering.

But there was an even greater fear now. The moon was full and the waxing gibbous past. It marked the second time Regana had missed her moon time.

The first time, she had been sure it was the stress of the upcoming battle and the fear of being discovered in their deception. By the night Jörg went to the Stone with the others, she had been secretly hopeful, imagining that not even Gawen would raise a hand to Jörg if there was a child involved. In the three weeks since that night, Regana had denied the possibility, even to herself. Now she could no longer deny it. Regana was undone, and not even Gawen could save her, she was sure.

She'd considered telling him several times, but every time, Regana felt as if her heart would burst if she uttered the damning words to him. He'd assured her over and over that there was nothing she could not tell him, but this went beyond anything Gawen was prepared for, she was sure.

Not to mention, the villagers would make no distinction between a child of Jörg, the Warrior, and a child of Veriel, the beast elder. Her life would be forfeit, if the father was known, and how could it not be? This was a problem, as Gawen had surmised the morning after the battle, which would only get bigger with time.

Regana stared at the dark sky morosely. If she had told Jörg that she had missed her moon time, would he still have gone to the Stone? She supposed it didn't matter now. Not really.

Drawing a cloak around her, Regana looked back at the empty house she was leaving behind. She needed a walk in the night air. If Jörg came to her, she'd ask for answers. If he didn't— It made no difference, she supposed. Regana wasn't even sure what she wanted to ask him except a hopeless 'why.'

What would Jörg say if he knew about the child she carried? What would he do? He had no kinder emotions to love it or her. Still, nothing Jörg did, even to killing them, would be worse than what she already faced, she surmised.

Regana stepped out into the darkness and darted up the path to their tree. Even in the trees, there was enough light from the full moon to see clearly, not that she had need of a lamp. She had traveled this path many nights without one. What was one more? On all but the darkest of nights, Regana could navigate her way through the paths to the clearing and to Jörg's chamber without a light to walk with. It had seemed their salvation at the time. Now she cursed it.

The clearing opened ahead of her, and she looked at the great tree through bitter tears. "Jörg?" Regana called out.

There was no answer.

She curled up at the base of the tree, determined to wait all night if she had to. Or until Gawen came to drag her home, she reminded herself. Either way, Regana would have to tell Gawen about the child soon, if she could just make her mouth form the words.

A rustling over her shoulder drew her attention.

"Jörg?" she called again.

But it wasn't Jörg who stepped from the trees. It was Tilbrand. Resten, she reminded herself as she launched to her feet and bolted down the path the way she had come. He moved as a flash, faster even than Gawen in training. Regana backed away from him as he stopped down the trail from her. Resten advanced on her, looking hungry and dangerous.

"What troubles you, Regana? I simply want what was promised me," he crooned.

"Promised?" she squeaked as she backed into the great tree. "What promise?"

"Marclef promised we would retain our rights if we gave him victory in battle. We did that. Now the night of choosing is upon us. I came to make my choice."

"No," she breathed. Regana clenched her fists against the rough bark to still the shaking that started at his suggestion.

"You gave your word. You agreed to marry any of the thirteen who chose you."

"You're not a Warrior," she countered uneasily.

"I was promised my rights," he growled as he approached her.

"I have Gawen's blessing. You cannot touch me," she warned, hoping to drive him off.

He hesitated for only a moment before his eyes hardened. "I will find a way to rip it from your throat," he vowed.

Resten jerked back as he reached for her, but the push of the amulet never materialized. He opened his mouth in a mute scream as long claws, wet with his foul blood, extended through his chest. As Resten was lifted up and away from her, Jörg took shape behind him. His face was set in fury, and his eyes shone silver beneath the moonlight.

Jörg glanced at Regana, then turned his attention back to his foe. "I warned you that I would never allow you to touch her," he growled as he dropped the beast at his feet only to grab him up by the hair with a hand now pristine and perfect.

"You can't kill me," Resten breathed. "It is not permitted."

"I can give you pain," Jörg promised. "I can give you pain such as you've never dreamed possible. And I will see you dead very soon. It is not an impossible thing." He turned his silver eyes to Regana again. "Go home. Leave here."

"No," she breathed.

He looked at her miserably. "Regana, I do not wish for you to see what I am now. I do not want you to see what I must do."

"I cannot go yet."

"He heals, Regana. I must act quickly," Jörg urged her.

She shook her head, adamant that she wouldn't leave while there was a chance at the answers she sought.

His jaw clenched down in anger. "As you wish," he decided.

Regana sucked in her breath, as Jörg's teeth lengthened into killing fangs. "No. You can't do it," she cried in distress, as his intent became clear.

Her stomach lurched, as he fell on Resten, tearing at his throat. The sound of his feeding made her physically ill. Jörg's eyes closed in something akin to pleasure as he stole the lifeblood from Resten. Regana wrapped her arms around her stomach, shaking in the shock of seeing him like this.

Jörg pulled his head back. The foul, dark blood on his fangs and dripping from his chin made her stomach clench. Regana fought to remain conscious despite her mind's rebellion in the face of the idea.

"I did not want this, Regana, but this is what I am now. There is no turning back from here. Please, do not look at me that way. Go now—I beg of you."

She backed against the trunk of the tree, incapable of answering, incapable of doing more than simply willing her heart to beat, her body to breathe, and her eyes to stay open to the sight as he returned to his feeding.

This was not Jörg. This was the beast Veriel. Her child had no father. Regana would never admit that the soulless beast before her had any connection to the precious life in her womb. She couldn't.

* * * *

Pauwel barreled toward the sound of Regana's cry, barely breathing in his panic. Veriel! It was undoubtedly Veriel come for her because he thought her unguarded.

Trees whipped at his face and chest as he crashed up the narrow track. Pauwel prayed that her amulet was intact. If the beast could not touch her until they arrived, he would give almost anything in return. To find her unharmed would even be worth giving his life in her defense.

He ground to a halt as a clearing opened before him. Regana stood, her back pressed to a tree, shaken and looking in horror at the two beasts before her.

Veriel raised his head, blood running in thick rivulets off his chin and splashing in heavy drops on Resten's face. He smiled a humorless smile. "Lord Kreuzträger, you have arrived just in time." He threw the beast in his hands toward Pauwel in disdain. "Kill that while it is weakened. Do not let it go to ground and heal. It is not worth the pain of weakening again."

Gawen crashed out next to Pauwel and launched toward Veriel, but the younger Warrior stopped him.

"Protect Regana," Pauwel ordered.

Gawen nodded without a thought of who should be ordering whom. When he had placed his larger body between Regana and Veriel, Pauwel strode forward, feeling the *Blutjagd* take hold in full force. His entire being cried out for Veriel's blood.

Veriel smiled in amusement as he came, his face now clean and boyishly handsome again. "Why come for me, Kreuzträger? Take Resten's life. He is the one who will come for your women, again and again, until he is dead."

Pauwel glanced at the downed beast, barely moving in his dire state. He hesitated. Chances like this would not come often. He delivered a blow to the beast's heart and took his throat on the way back to his feet.

Pauwel hesitated again at Regana's groan. She buried her face in her hands, weaving on her feet. He glared at Veriel and stepped over Resten's body toward him.

Veriel put up a hand to still Pauwel's advance on him. "Hold, Kreuzträger. Tonight is not our time. I will go now. Guard Regana well, Gawen. There are much worse beasts than myself to protect her from, as tonight shows."

He sighed and looked over Gawen's shoulder at Regana's tear-stained face. "I'm sorry, Regana. You know what I am now. Never come to this place again. I am not what I was, and the others are worse." Veriel shook his head and growled out several curses as Regana turned from him. He nodded to Pauwel and faded away.

The young lord looked at the empty space in shock. His senses told him nothing. Pauwel turned several times, scanning for any sign of attack, but none came.

Still, for all he knew, Veriel remained in the spot where he once stood—or behind the tree Regana huddled by. Wherever he was, Pauwel had no way of predicting it.

He locked his gaze on Regana. She looked shocked and frightened in light of Gawen's rage. Her brother had her by the arm, venting his displeasure at her while she all but cowered from him. Pauwel's heart softened as he watched her. She'd had enough. Couldn't Gawen see that?

When her brother smoothed her hair, he knew that the older man had found his control again.

"Gawen, we should get her in," he half suggested, half ordered.

The master trainer looked around suspiciously, suddenly aware as Pauwel was that they could not predict the next attack. He nodded and swept Regana to him as he turned.

* * * *

Gawen grabbed Regana by her arm and swung her around to face him. He towered over her, and she shrank from him as if she expected him to strike her. On some level, that fear angered him. On another, she was not far from the truth of his state of mind.

"What were you thinking?" he demanded. "Explain this!"

"I just...wanted to take a walk. I have my amulet," she managed weakly.

The urge to shake her was almost overwhelming, and his hand tightened around her upper arm as he fought to control his urges. "In the night? You must never leave the house after nightfall. Not without me."

Regana nodded silently and lowered her eyes in a way most uncharacteristic for her. Gawen stilled. Something was very wrong here. He smoothed her hair back from her face in concern, in their ritual of healing.

"Gawen," Pauwel called to him. "We should get her in."

Gawen scanned the area, nodded, and wrapped an arm around his sister protectively, leading her back to the house with Pauwel at their backs. Tremors seemed to race within Regana's body as she walked.

"We will talk inside," he assured her.

She shot him a look that he could only classify as fearful before casting her gaze down at the path again.

"Regana, what is wrong?"

She met his eyes and looked as if she was about to say something. His heart nearly stopped in relief. Then Regana closed her eyes with a tortured expression and shook her head before returning to her survey of the ground before her. Gawen sighed and swept her into the main room. She didn't fight him when he seated her in a chair by the fire, but she didn't meet his eyes.

His arms crossed over his chest, he stared down at the top of her head. Regana was making herself as small as possible in the chair and studiously avoiding him.

"Regana, what were you doing in the woods?"

"A walk," she mumbled.

"A lie," he countered.

She shook her head slowly.

"What did Veriel say to you?"

She shot another fearful look at him before staring into the fire. "He ordered me to leave while he handled

Resten. He didn't want me to look at him, to see what he is now."

"Why?"

Regana shrugged.

"Why didn't you leave?"

"I wanted to know why..." She faltered and shook her head.

"You were baiting a beast?" he asked incredulously.

"He's not!" Regana met his eyes angrily, swallowed, then looked away. "He can't be, but he is," she decided miserably.

Gawen sighed and sank into the chair across from her. "I know you and Jörg were friends, but he is not Jörg any longer," he told her quietly. "He's not human, Regana."

"Neither are you," she spat.

"I'm not damned. Cursed, but not damned. He chose—" he tried to explain.

"I don't believe that," she whispered. "He had no reason."

"Fear of death is a powerful thing."

"He wasn't afraid of death."

"You can't know that," Gawen reasoned with her.

"I know," she replied with a conviction that made him nervous.

"How, Regana?"

She shot a guarded look at him, as if something lay just beneath the surface of her. Regana rose to storm away, but Gawen caught her by the wrist and started to pull her back. She was shaking like a tree limb in a high wind now. Why would she fear him, of all people?

He looked at Pauwel out of the corner of his eye and noted that the young Warrior was making himself inconspicuous in the dark corners of the room. Regana seemed to have forgotten he was there, and Gawen had no wish to lose the tenuous cracks he was seeing in her shell. He turned his attention back to her without asking the other man to leave.

"How could you know that, Regana?"

She took a deep breath. "I can't," she admitted, but in a tone that didn't ease his apprehension. "I couldn't, could I?" Something burned in her eyes, not quite a challenge but proud and somewhat defiant.

"But, you are adamant in your belief that he was not afraid of death?"

She lowered her eyes and didn't answer.

"Regana," he barked.

"Jörg would never," she began miserably.

Gawen sighed. "What was there between you and Veriel?"

"Nothing," she proclaimed in horror.

He furrowed his brow. Perhaps, the difference for her was in a complete separation of the man and the beast. Gawen wondered if he had simply asked the question in a way that repelled her somehow.

"What was between you and Jörg, then?" he asked in irritation.

Regana didn't answer, and she refused to raise her head. Gawen felt his anger rising dangerously. He would have to leave her so as not to hurt her if he came to no conclusion soon. Gawen stood, gripping her wrist tightly so that she could not bolt from him, and cupped her chin to raise her face to him. His heart took up a choppy rhythm.

She was crying. Silent, heartbreaking tears stained her cheeks. "Jörg would never choose that path," she assured him quietly. "Not willingly. He was tricked into it somehow. I know it, and he confirms it. This was not his choice."

"Tricked or not, it's done. It's over."

Regana swallowed again and nodded. "May I go, Gawen?"

He tried to meet her eyes, but she avoided him studiously. She ran her fingers over the scar on her hand nervously.

"What was the blood oath you took?" he asked, suddenly sure that it was vital to her upset.

She didn't meet his eyes. Regana didn't seem to breathe for a moment. "That we would wed no one but each other," she admitted.

"He's holding you to that?" Gawen asked. "You were a child, and even then, you claimed he had tricked you into the oath."

Regana shook her head, half swallowing another sob. "He freed me from it the night Sibold... He told me that he had made many promises in his life, and there were only certain ones he could honor now. I knew what he meant." She shook as she admitted it.

Gawen searched the Stone for answers, sure that he had uncovered what he needed to know, but it was still silent.

He sensed her in frustration, not sure that it would tell him anything he could use. He had never used it on anyone but the women provided for their needs, so he had no idea if it would tell him the depth of their relationship. Could it tell Gawen if she was intact? He resisted asking that question outright, sure that he would spook Regana and she would close herself off from him again.

He groaned in understanding. Her body was not on a cycle. "Sit down, Regana," he ordered sharply.

She hesitated for just a moment, then took her seat again. Regana met his eyes nervously. She hadn't told him. Was this what she felt she couldn't tell him?

"Tell me the truth," Gawen demanded. "Is the child Jörg's?"

Her eyes widened. She paled, weaving, then righting herself.

"Is it?" he asked more gently. "You must tell me."

Gawen no longer cared that Pauwel was there. The entire village would know that she carried when she started to show. There would be no hiding this. *It will only become more of a problem in time—*

"Yes," she admitted in a low, sad voice. Regana ran the palms of her hands over her stomach protectively.

"Why did you do this?"

"I loved him," she answered miserably.

"Does he know? Does anyone know?"

Regana shook her head. "When h-he—" she hitched out through trembling lips. "I wasn't certain yet. A-after, it was too late."

Gawen seethed at Veriel's incompetence. He met Pauwel's speculative look in surprise. "What are you thinking?" he demanded.

"We can protect her from this," he decided.

"How?" Gawen stormed. "This is not something we can hide. Veriel will figure it out eventually...or the villagers."

Regana flinched as he said the beast's name.

"Will they? If she were wed, a baby would be the expected outcome. Is Veriel watching so closely that he would realize? And need anyone else know that Veriel was involved in any way? Her baby could be her husband's child, if it is presented that way."

"Wed to who?" Gawen snapped.

"I've not made my choice yet," Pauwel reminded him.

"No," Regana stormed. "I cannot be your duty."

Gawen stared at him, his mind numbed by shock. "Pauwel, I cannot allow this," he replied weakly.

Was the young Warrior really so heartbroken for his lost chosen one that he would consider this course? Still, was Pauwel so far printed that Regana could not take the place of the one he'd lost in time? If he were so printed, Pauwel would eventually have to renege on this course or die.

"I cannot allow it," Gawen repeated, cursing himself for considering Regana's well being before that of this honorable young man who was willing to accept her dishonor for her.

"You must. The alternative is unacceptable," he stated calmly.

Gawen sighed. The villagers would kill Regana, if the father of her child were known, and he could not allow his sister to die for such a mistake as this, no matter how monumental a blunder it had been. "You're right, of course," he conceded wearily.

"No," Regana repeated. "I will not be bound to any man for his honor and duty."

"You want this baby, Regana? Do you want the child to live? And yourself?"

She looked away with tears in her eyes.

"Then you must accept what we must do to protect you."

"A child of—Jörg would undoubtedly be a powerful Warrior," Pauwel noted carefully. "Born into another house and raised as part of it, the child need never know his true parentage."

"You would raise him as if he were your own?" Gawen asked. If Pauwel could not accept the child and do so, it would all be for naught.

"He would wear my seal and be my heir," Pauwel offered honestly. "I would nurture him and train him. He would be as one of my own children. You have my vow on that. If I do this, no one will ever know that he is anything but a child of mine."

"Regana?" Gawen asked for her acceptance. If she could not go to him willingly, disaster would ensue.

She looked at Pauwel uncertainly, then dropped her gaze away. "What about..."

Gawen could see the blush come up on her cheeks clearly. "He'll be your husband, Regana," he thundered.

"I would never take an unwilling woman, Regana," Pauwel answered quietly. "You have my word on that, as well."

Regana looked at him in surprise and nodded.

"Pauwel, you cannot make an agreement like that," Gawen protested.

"As long as she presents as a married woman would, I will manage. Do you agree?" he asked her.

"I do," she answered quietly. "I will present the pretense of a married woman."

Pauwel nodded. "Then Thorald will join us tomorrow."

"Tomorrow?" Regana protested, panic touching her voice.

The young Warrior smiled crookedly. "We are a young couple in love," he countered. "What would happen if I did not claim you immediately? We must secure our union as soon as possible—for the child's sake."

"We'll have to convince Thorald that this is truly Regana's choice before he will consent to join you," Gawen noted. "That should not be overly difficult. Convincing him to join you immediately will be more difficult."

"He will consent. I will tell him that I am well into printing, and he must, by virtue of my need and her wish, join us now. Thorald is a reasonable man."

Chapter Six

Regana looked around Pauwel's house, the house she would share with him, in apprehension. She jumped slightly as her husband—she tested the word— brushed past her.

He looked at her sadly. "I'll show you where you can put your things," he offered.

She nodded and followed him into the larger bedchamber.

Pauwel dropped her small bundle onto a chest. "You may use this," he told her. "Some of my mother's things are still in it. Use any of it you wish."

"Thank you, Pauwel," she replied. "You are most kind."

"It is not kind to provide for a wife. It is expected that I would do so," he informed her.

"I thank you anyway."

Pauwel nodded slowly. "This is our chamber."

"Together?" Regana asked in shock, before she could get a handle on her tongue. Of course, together. Why would they sleep apart? That was a thing for Kings, not for common lords of the Stone.

He sighed. "We must present as a married couple. Kethe sleeps in the other chamber." Pauwel paused and met her eyes. "You gave your word," he reminded her quietly.

Regana nodded. "Yes, I did. It is fine, Pauwel," she assured him.

He smiled tightly. "Good. Then we can do this." He seemed strangely tense, and he avoided looking at her directly. "Kethe will be here soon," he commented.

"Why don't you get settled in? I must go train with Gawen and the others."

She smiled tentatively. "Watch out for Gawen's left back slice," she warned. "He likes to sneak it in behind a right thrust."

Pauwel looked at her in surprise. "Yes, I know it well. I will be careful." He moved as if to touch her cheek, then he looked at his hand and dropped it to her arm instead. "I will return to share the evening meal with you. It smells as if Kethe has a stew on. You should," he glanced at her midsection and away again, "eat some, please."

"I will."

Pauwel nodded and lowered his hand to his side. "Good," he repeated. For a single, tense moment, he stared at her before he turned on his heel and strode away.

Regana watched him go, willing her body to unwind. She uttered several dark curses that she was sure Gawen would disapprove of as the front door swung shut behind Pauwel, her husband.

She pressed her hands to her stomach miserably. Her wedding night was supposed to be a very different affair: a different place, a different man, and some hope of love in her future. Now her baby and a living lie were all that were left to her.

Regana packed her things into the chest Pauwel had provided for her, pausing to run her hand over the clothing already inside. Her breath caught in her throat. The pieces may be old, but they were stunning. They were a collection of beautiful reds and blues in fine fabrics, accented with rich trims and fur.

An amber pendant lay on top. Regana shook her head. Such a precious family jewel should be Kethe's. It was not for a woman like Regana, only brought here out of a sense of duty and kinship to her brother. She closed the chest and moved away.

She settled on the high bed, set on a low dais against the far wall of the room. Regana would share the bed with her husband this night, a relative stranger offering protection for herself and her child. He was offering her safety and respectability, and she was being selfish to ask for more than that, she decided.

Regana sighed and scanned her surroundings with a critical eye. The etching on the bed caught her attention, and she ran a hand over it in awe of the craftsmanship.

"Pauwel made it himself," a voice behind her explained.

Regana snapped a startled look at Kethe and took to her feet in embarrassment.

"He made it for his wedding night. I am sure that he didn't tell you," she teased, while Regana felt her cheeks darken. "I'm sorry. I didn't mean to startle you."

That was so like Kethe, she remembered. The woman was apologizing to an interloper in her home. Would that Regana had ever been half as proper and gentle a lady as Kethe was she would not be in this mess now.

"No. It is fine, Kethe." Regana turned her gaze back to the etching. "It's very good," she noted in a more confident tone.

"He's been working on it for over a year."

"Oh..." Regana felt her stomach knot painfully at the thought. Pauwel had put all that work and hope into his wedding bed, and now he was sharing it with her instead of his chosen—whoever so foolish a woman was. She felt sick at what he had given up for her.

"Come. I saw Pauwel on his way to train. He ordered me to see that you eat. I notice that he was right and you have not done so of your own accord."

"I'm not very hungry just now, Kethe. Thank you anyway," she managed. In truth, Regana felt as if she would bring back anything she attempted at that point.

"It was an order." The older woman smiled. "I don't know about you, but I've found it unwise to ignore Pauwel's orders."

Regana looked at her apprehensively. Was that the sort of man she'd tied herself to? A man to fear?

Kethe laughed as she took the young bride's arm. "A joke, Regana," she assured her. "Surely, you know better than anyone how gentle Pauwel is."

* * * *

Ditrich hit the floor hard, and Gawen winced at the bruises it would leave.

"Hold," he called. "Pauwel, sheathe and attend!"

The young man sheathed his weapons and turned to follow Gawen out into the clear day outside. Pauwel was one of the few Warriors skilled enough to fight dual style. Only Gawen himself and Veriel had joined him in following Sibold's path in that regard. The other Warriors all fought standard. The training for dual was much more vigorous and the handling of two blades required much more control, a step that never seemed to apply to Veriel. His blades seemed literal extensions of his hands, much like they truly were now.

But Pauwel was his problem now. Gawen had never seen the young Warrior train this vigorously before, and his control seemed strained.

"Explain," Gawen requested as cordially as he could.

Pauwel shrugged, then shivered in the release of his *Blutjagd*. "I don't want them to get cocky. After all, if they take me, they will think themselves capable of taking an elder. Even I only defeated an injured one, a weakened one. Why must we make so much of this, Gawen?"

The master trainer sighed. "They need hope. They need to believe that we can win this. If we can kill them, we have a chance."

Pauwel nodded his agreement and turned his face to a thick stand of trees. "I just don't like deceiving them," he admitted. "I can't be sure that I would have defeated Resten alone. If Veriel hadn't—"

"Do not speak his name to me," Gawen growled out, cutting him off.

Pauwel shook his head sadly.

The older man sighed. "Things are going well with Regana?" he asked.

"Very well," he replied simply.

He eyed the younger man suspiciously. Pauwel's jaw was set tight and his muscles bunched beneath the sleeves of his tunic.

"Pauwel, you do not have to do this."

"Yes, I do." He said it quietly, calmly.

"If you find yourself printing on a woman, save your sanity and return my sister to my care. There will be no dishonor for you. We will simply explain the burn, that it was all a mistake," he finished.

"It will never come to that," Pauwel asserted. "Even if it drives me mad, I will never send Regana away."

"You must. If it comes to that, send her away and save your soul."

"It will not come to that," he repeated. He met Gawen's eyes, looking determined and angry. "I'm for home. I think the others have had enough of my arm today. Besides that, what would they think of me if I did not run to my bride at my first opportunity?"

"Keep my offer in mind."

Pauwel glared at him as he swept past.

Gawen watched him stalk away. How had he let himself get talked into this? Pauwel was skirting the edges of madness, all because Gawen had not been strong enough to find a way to save Regana that didn't involve risking the young Warrior.

* * * *

Pauwel forced his hands to unfist as he left Gawen far behind. What a damned ridiculous situation he had gotten himself into. Cuckolded before he could even claim his chosen bride and giving her a promise not to touch her just to get her to wed him. He growled at the stupidity of the entire situation.

He knew Regana was fond of watching the men train, but Pauwel had never considered that she was watching anyone in particular. She had been careful not to show a preference.

Or had she? He slowed his step as he considered it. Regana watched the men training dual most avidly.

At the time, Pauwel had assumed she was drawn by the excitement of the two-bladed style. In retrospect, she had probably been watching Jörg and Gawen all that time.

Pauwel ground his teeth at his own foolish pride. How many times had he sought out a fight in her line of sight to try to draw her attention? How many times had he misread a kindly smile from her? How many nights had he dreamed of claiming Regana after the battle or fantasized her beneath him as he lay with one of the women provided for their needs?

All that time, she had been in Jörg's bed, releasing the need in that damned pup that had all but driven Pauwel himself to madness. He groaned in the knowledge that she loved Jörg. It would be easier to convince her to turn a kind eye to himself if she were not pining for another man she could never have.

The fact that Jörg took her before the battle was almost forgivable. Pauwel had walked the edges of insanity many nights. Slipping over the edge wouldn't have been difficult. All it would have taken was a kind word from Regana at the wrong moment to ensure his own fall.

The first unforgivable thing Jörg had done was taking her—*ever, even once!*—without making sure she wasn't in high cycle. He could not have been so cocky as to think himself invulnerable. His death could have occurred in battle easily, leaving Regana alone and with child without the benefit of Jörg's protection. While Gawen would have demanded the child's rights of inheritance and likely been granted it, it would still have been an unconscionable hardship to submit her to.

Worse, Jörg hadn't died. His outright death would have been kinder to all involved. Leaving her the way he did, child or no, had left Regana questioning why, lost in self-blame, and dishonored in the worst possible way.

Did she still dare hope that Veriel was not the beast all knew him to be? That he might harbor some kind emotion for her and her unborn child? He shuddered at the thought.

The baby had been a shock to him. For a torturous moment, Pauwel had considered turning his back on her and walking away. Then the familiar burn had set in, and he'd known his course. The baby may have been an accident of Jörg, but it was part of Regana. The regret that Pauwel had not put it in her womb himself was immaterial compared to the possibilities of the joy of placing the next, and he could see the child as an extension of Regana until he forged love for it on his own terms.

He would have promised anything to get Regana to accept him as husband and father to her child. When she agreed, Pauwel had almost wept in relief.

Now she awaited him at his home, an unwilling bride that viewed him as a duty and a means to the end of safeguarding herself and her child. Worse, Regana feared him. She shied from his every touch.

Pauwel sighed. Having her in his bed and still not touching her would mean madness for him, but as long as his brothers put the mad animal in him to death after Pauwel had convinced all of the baby's claim to his estate, he will have done all he could for the only woman he could love. And, if the gods showed him the ultimate mercy and Regana turned a favorable eye to him before that time came, his soul would sing for the rest of his life. Pauwel was too far into printing to do any less for her. He hadn't lied to Thorald about that.

He eased the door open and steeled himself before entering. Pauwel came in slowly and followed the sound of voices to Kethe's chamber. He smiled at the sight of them sitting together and talking. He stayed silent so as not to disturb them. At least, Regana would have Kethe to bring her peace here. He was glad for it.

"You're being ridiculous," Regana asserted. "Why can't I help? I must earn my keep here somehow."

"Oh, you'll earn it," Kethe teased boldly.

Before Pauwel could roar out his anger at the impertinence of such a statement, Regana buried her face in her hands. If only Kethe hadn't said such a thing. He would never win her, if Regana continued to be so upset at the notion of intimacy with him.

"I am undone, and you think it funny," Regana groaned.

Pauwel's blood ran cold. Regana could not— No! She would not tell Kethe that. She understood as well as anyone what was at stake if the truth were known.

"Nonsense," Kethe replied. "If anyone is undone, it is my hot-blooded brother. It is lucky for him that Gawen decided to grant his blessing and not take his head for this trespass."

Pauwel let out his breath in relief, as his wife started speaking again.

"He didn't have much of a choice, I suppose."

That much was true. Pauwel had played on Gawen's fear to get his permission.

"And this is hardly Pauwel's fault," Regana defended him hotly. "Please, Kethe. Do not vilify him in this."

"Still, I owe him harsh words for not being honest with me," Kethe countered. "When you swooned while drawing water, I nearly joined you in fear."

"She what?" Pauwel thundered from the doorway.

Regana stood and spun to face him with a frantic look on her face. Too quickly, he noted. He was a blur of movement as he saw the color drain from her face, and he caught her smoothly as her balance deserted her.

Pauwel swept Regana up in his arms and headed for his own bed. "Kethe, fetch a cool cloth," he ordered.

She scrambled ahead of him as he turned into the other room. Pauwel lay Regana on the bed with her knees up on his leg to raise them slightly and rubbed her hands to help her blood move more naturally. Regana looked at him in concern and started to rise. He pushed her back gently with one large hand to her shoulder.

"Pauwel," she began.

"Stay there," he growled. "Drawing water? You're mad."

Regana watched him warily, sinking back into the mattress, as if he was a danger to her somehow. "Other women—"

"Other women are not my wife. Kethe will make sure you rest from now on." Pauwel barely registered the panic that tinged his concern for her. "I will not allow you to risk yourself—or my child."

Her eyes widened, and she flicked them toward the doorway as if she expected Kethe to be standing there watching the scene unfold. "Your..." She stopped uncertainly.

"My wife and my child," he repeated. "You will not endanger either one." Pauwel met her eyes, and his heart softened. "I couldn't bear it. Do you understand that?"

She swallowed hard and nodded, tears misting her dark eyes. "I understand. It will be as you wish. You have my word."

"Good enough." He took the cloth from Kethe's hand and settled it on Regana's forehead. He met Kethe's smirk with a hard glare, and she returned to her room without comment. "Close your eyes and rest a few moments," he crooned to Regana.

Pauwel watched her long after her eyes fluttered shut, confused at his reaction. Women carrying a child did not require such coddling, and he knew it. Still, some mad part of him demanded such care with her and— *My baby. Ours! Mine! Not simply Regana's and never Jörg's.* She was his and so was the baby she carried. Nothing would be permitted to threaten that, while he lived to prevent it.

* * * *

Regana pulled the covers around her hips and waited nervously for Pauwel to come to his bed. She wasn't sure if he had stayed with her the entire time she'd slept that afternoon, but he had still been watching her when she woke.

His eyes had been disconcerting, soft and shimmering like warm, black liquid. His eyes drew her, and she'd had to look away. Even now, those eyes haunted her.

She berated herself soundly. When had she left all semblance of decency behind? Regana barely knew anything of Pauwel Lord Kreuzträger though she'd known him practically from her birth. At least she had grown with Jörg. Not that the fact excused her wanton behavior, but she had no idea what to expect of the man she had to pretend was the father of her child, that she had to share a bed with.

Not that Regana could claim to know what Jörg was capable of either. The moment when his madness had taken hold of him still haunted her. When his body lay over her, crushing her into the grass beneath, and his mouth claimed hers, her first reaction had been fear.

The moment had come out of nowhere. Jörg had come to the clearing while she was relaxing there and sat to talk with her. Regana remembered smiling at him in answer to some teasing comment he made before he had her under him, his hands pulling at her dress and his eyes strange and fierce, as if not possessed of his senses. The first time had been quick, her cry of pain muted in his mouth, as her fingers fisted in his tunic.

Jörg hadn't paused but had continued to master her, his seed easing the way for him. Her fear had subsided, as he'd muttered endearments and pleas between the motions of his hands and the possessions of his mouth. The printing, she understood. Jörg would have died without her. He'd needed her to retain his sanity. If he'd waited for the choosing ceremony after the battle, he would not have survived.

In the end, her shocked inability to act had given way to her acceptance of what he was doing to her. In time, Regana had come to revel in his inability to control his need for her. Jörg could not wait to see her unclothed. He could not wait to claim her with his body.

He'd taken her there beneath their tree and laid gentle kisses over Regana when it was over, professing his love to her. It wasn't until later that Jörg seemed to realize the full import of what he had done, but he'd assured her of his love and his intention to marry her.

That moment, when he'd fallen on her under the tree to claim her without reason, Regana had been sure she didn't know him at all, though she'd reasoned later that it was only the madness she hadn't known and not the man. When Jörg went to the Stone after all his promises and assurances, she had been sure she hadn't known him at all.

Now she was married to a man she truly did not know, and—Gods help her! Regana wanted to be a real wife to him. As if he'd have her!

She considered her life miserably. Giving herself to Jörg got her into this mess, but she wasn't so sure throwing herself at Pauwel would make it better. He'd never given any indication that he wanted more than the marriage of convenience he'd contracted for. Even if Pauwel did, what would he think of her if she threw herself at him?

A harlot, Regana realized sadly. As if she wasn't proof of that already.

She had resigned herself to that sad state when she hadn't screamed at Jörg's handling. Regana had resigned herself to that when she began to enjoy the things Jörg was doing and the power her body had over him. She'd given up all decency when she'd started going to him willingly, allowing him to sate his needs in her without remorse for the laws she was breaking to do so. She'd lost all decency when she'd decided her love for him was more important to her than morals.

Regana would have lied for him. She had lied for him more than once. Worse, she'd decided that what they had was more important than the possibility that Gawen would take Jörg's life for it. It bothered her, but she'd still allowed it to continue and even urged it to continue despite that fact.

Like it or not, Regana couldn't act on this mindless attraction she felt for Pauwel. Was she such a wanton that the first man who looked kindly on her after Jörg left her bed had her in such a state? Regana laughed at the irony of it. She was married to a man who was honorable and caring, a man who made her heart race, and she couldn't even express how much she wanted a real marriage with him.

She startled, as Pauwel stepped into the room, pulling the covers to her chest. He took in the sight of her, and she met his eyes, burning too brightly in his half-shadowed face. Regana looked away, aware of what he must see in her. She watched him through her eyelashes. Pauwel nodded grimly and closed the door behind him. He moved to the bed in the almost non-existent light and disrobed quietly. She felt the bed sink, as his weight settled onto it lightly, and she held her breath.

"Lie down, Regana. Get comfortable. I told you that I don't take unwilling women. I didn't lie to you," he whispered.

She let out her breath slowly and sank to the bed. What had seemed like a huge bed that morning suddenly seemed cramped with Pauwel's form sharing the space with her. It was impossible to move without touching him, and every touch made her want to touch him again.

It was like finding your way after your lamp died out. Her cheek brushed the muscles of his arm and she tried to move further away. Her hand connected with the nude expanse of his thigh, and Regana jerked away in shock, abruptly and acutely aware of his state of complete undress.

"Regana," he growled under his breath.

She stilled immediately. "I'm sorry. I am unaccustomed to sharing a bed with a man." Regana groaned as she considered how ridiculous that sounded coming from her mouth. "I mean," she began miserably.

"I know what you mean," he grumbled. "If touching me is so horrible for you, we'll figure something out."

"It's not horrible," she countered in a whisper. It wasn't, and that was part of the problem. "I mean..." Regana gave up and swore fluently under her breath.

Pauwel jerked in surprise. "Where did you learn that?"

"At training. Several of the men are eloquent in their usage."

Regana held her breath, waiting to see what his response would be, and was shocked when he chuckled.

"I suppose they are," he conceded. "Well, I will inform them that such things are inappropriate around a lady such as yourself before the next time you come to training."

She froze. Pauwel had said it honestly enough. There didn't seem to be an underlying snub in his comment about her character.

In a moment of clarity, Regana realized that it was nothing more than the appearance he would fabricate for them both. "You wish me to go to training?" she asked, her heart aching that it was nothing but a casted play.

"I would much appreciate it if you did," he answered. There was something cautious in that, as if he thought she might refuse him...or he was testing her agreement.

"Very well. I will accompany you tomorrow."

"No. I want you to rest tomorrow. The following day will be soon enough. Agreed?"

"As you wish."

"Now, will you relax? If you don't find touching me horrible, and I don't find your touch horrible, can we sleep in peace?"

"Sleep well, Pauwel."

Regana lay awake—and very still for long after his breathing normalized into a deep, peaceful rhythm. When she was sure that he was fully asleep, she relaxed against his shoulder and dropped off to sleep.

Chapter Seven

Pauwel drifted into a warm, semi-conscious state, aware that daybreak had passed but too comfortable to consider starting his day. A movement against his chest caught his attention, and he lay very still, searching his memory for an explanation.

A pulse of pleasure gripped him as the answer came to him. *Regana.* His wife was in his bed with him.

He opened his eyes, praying his body wasn't imagining the glorious sensations he was experiencing. During the night, she had curled into his shoulder. The warm, soft length of her lay along his side and her knee rested lightly on his thigh.

Pauwel's heart beat frantically behind his ribs as he placed his hand over her hip gently. He drank in the feminine scent of her, and his body tightened in response. He ground his teeth in restraint as the burn in his blood reached a fever pitch, demanding he claim her properly and be done with this torture.

The knock on the chamber door came without warning, and Regana startled in response. Her eyes widened as her position became clear to her, and she started to push away from him.

He tightened his hand around her slightly and bent his head to whisper next to her ear. "Be still. We will use this to present the first of many scenes." In truth, Pauwel didn't care about the scene. He simply wanted an excuse to keep her in his arms and bed as long as he could manage.

Her struggle ceased. Regana nodded and sank back to her nest against him. He brushed his beard through her hair, laying his lips to the silken strands as he laid back.

"Come in," Pauwel invited.

Kethe popped her head around the door and smiled a knowing smile at the scene before her. "Ditrich and Gawen came to fetch you on their way to train, but I sent them away. They do expect to see you sometime today," she teased.

"Soon, Kethe," he crooned, drinking in the look in Regana's eyes.

He could feel her nervous wriggling, but he could also smell her arousal. It may frighten her, but there was a definite chance for a true marriage with her. He thanked several of the ancient gods and the new god of his grandfather for their mercy on his soul in granting that wish.

Kethe chuckled as she removed herself, closing the door carefully.

Regana sighed in relief. "She's gone," she reminded him, her fidgeting more pronounced.

"Is this so terrible?" Pauwel asked, drawing her closer to him, reluctant to release her so soon.

Regana closed her eyes and tried to calm her breathing as her breasts swelled against him. "No, it's not," she admitted.

"Good, because we will have to do this type of thing often. I'd like to think you don't dislike it too intensely."

"I don't," she whispered.

Pauwel felt a sudden urge to push the limits a little, to gauge her response to him. "It may be called for— I may have to kiss you from time to time. Would that be too uncomfortable for you?"

She looked at him in surprise, and her body stiffened. "Kiss? In public?" she asked in a nervous, little voice.

"Ah, that's right. Your—intimacy has always been private," he mused. "Let me show you." What was intended as a command came out a request.

Regana locked on his eyes, and he was afraid she would refuse him. Finally, she nodded in a jerky movement.

Pauwel turned to face her, moving his hand from her hip to her face. He cupped his fingers around her cheek and ran his thumb over her jaw and lips. Regana trembled at his touch, and her eyes dilated in shock, but he could feel her body temperature rise in response. He leaned his face to replace his thumb with his lips, teasing her with the feel of him without demanding anything in return.

At first, her lips hardened. Regana's hands locked against his chest like a shield, not pushing him away but keeping Pauwel at a constant distance. Her shield didn't relax, but her mouth softened beneath his in a mute surrender to his attentions.

Pauwel flicked his tongue lazily over her lips, tasting her. Regana shuddered against him and bit back a small sound in her throat. As he ran his tongue along the slight opening of her mouth, she melted against him and simultaneously granted him the access he craved.

Her tentative side fell aside abruptly, as his tongue surged forth into her waiting mouth. He startled in the realization that she was suddenly on familiar ground. Her reactions were hot and demanding, and Pauwel found himself torn.

Part of him wanted to follow the heat between them as far as it would lead immediately. Regana was obviously willing to give him this, and he needed it so very badly. Another part of him argued that such actions would make him not much better than Jörg had been.

Regana's reactions told a story. The impetuous pup had wronged her even more deeply than Pauwel had realized. He'd never taught her the sweet, slow, kind touch a man could use when making love to a woman. Demanding was all Regana knew, all Jörg had taught her.

For that reason alone, Pauwel could not be demanding. *Damn Jörg for this!*

He sobered. Jörg was damned, all right.

Pauwel cupped her face with both hands and slowed his pace to a torturous exploration of her. Regana matched his pace. She moved against him in a haze borne of passion. He pulled his face away and met her eyes solidly.

Regana searched his expression. She seemed to wilt into a hopeless unhappiness as she looked at him. She averted her gaze and wrapped her arms around her breasts, hard and heavy in her obvious excitement.

It took a moment for him to realize that she was stifling sobs. "Regana," he soothed her, touching her cheek gently.

She shrank from him, trembling, seemingly frightened of his touch.

"Please, tell me what's wrong. Have I hurt you somehow?" There had to be some reason for this response. What had he done wrong?

"No," she assured him in a broken voice, her shoulders quaking harder.

"Then what?"

"You deserve better," she choked out. "Why did you agree to this marriage? I know why I did, but why would you do this to yourself?"

"I don't understand." That was no lie. Nothing she was saying made sense to him.

"You're a good man, Pauwel. You deserve a real lady, not someone like me."

"Someone like—" He felt his temper start to burn. "I fail to see what you think is wrong with yourself," he growled.

Regana tensed in his arms, and Pauwel willed his voice to gentle. He was frightening her, and he had no urge to do that.

Pauwel forced himself on. "You made a mistake. You gave yourself to a man you loved. I can't speak for his feelings, but I know he didn't treat you the way he should have. I know he didn't show the proper concern and care for you. He took you, possessed you, but he never showed you tenderness. What I just did— You've never felt anything like it, have you?"

She looked at him in confusion. "I'm too bold. I curse like a man. You deserve a gentle lady," she argued, but it was a weak, uncertain thing, as if she was both sure and unsure that he would agree with her.

"You are bold only because that is all you were taught. Would it make you feel better if I forbid you to curse?"

Regana furrowed her brow.

"It wouldn't," he assured her.

She hesitated for a long moment, then managed a nod.

"Now, you may try to defend him to me, though I hope you do not, but I will tell you the truth of Jörg. He has wronged you in every conceivable way a man can wrong a willing woman right up to leaving you the way he did.

"You have nothing to feel guilty for. You trusted him to behave as an honorable man should have. He didn't. If I am reading your reactions to my overtures correctly, he never did. When he took your maidenhead—"

Regana startled and tried to push away, her breaths hitching violently, her eyes wide.

Pauwel dragged her back to his chest, stilling her flailing hands as gently as he could. "Don't," he breathed. "I am not Jörg."

She shook in his embrace, but her struggles ceased.

"Did he take you tenderly then, at least?"

Regana didn't reply.

"Did he?" he asked more forcefully, keeping his voice a mere whisper.

"It is supposed to hurt the first time," she replied. "I've always heard that."

There was something shamefully damning of Jörg in her insistence. So, he hadn't been tender and kind, even then. That stoked Pauwel's fury another notch. The need to have her list Jörg's crimes for him as judge beat at him.

"Yes, it hurts," he ground out, "but tenderness can minimize the pain. He didn't do that for you, did he?

Jörg was demanding. He was always demanding. Wasn't he?"

"He didn't... He was...t-too far," she stammered. "His printing was too far for it to be different. Please, you don't understand."

Pauwel stilled, his mind working on that damning statement. "He didn't ask your permission," he breathed. "He took you unwilling."

"He didn't ask my permission, but he didn't— He couldn't—" She closed her eyes, a pained expression on her face. "I loved him," she whispered, seemingly tortured by the admission. "I wanted..." Her eyes opened again. She faltered, pleading with him silently, as if she were uncertain what she'd wanted even now.

Gods, but she was confused. Pauwel started to question her several times but stopped himself, his mind rebelling at what she was saying. Jörg hadn't asked her permission, but she believed him incapable of it. She believed him gripped by madness and unable to be kind. What had she forgiven him? How heinous were his crimes?

"Unready, then," he ventured, praying he was wrong. It was the least courtesy Jörg had owed her, arousing her to accept him with a ready sheath for his cock. "Demanding and unready?"

Regana shuddered, no doubt reliving memories that were best forgotten. "I..." She squeezed her eyes shut, as if blocking them out of her mind.

The sour smell of true fear poured off her in waves, answering when she was unequal to it. There was little question that unready was an accurate description, that the very memory of the crime terrified Regana...even now.

Pauwel tried to push away visions of Jörg forcing himself into her dry body, taking what he wanted, using her maiden's blood to ease the way. Why had she not turned him over to Gawen? The answer was obvious. She'd loved Jörg, and was confused by his madness—perhaps frightened of what Jörg was capable of.

"He didn't even grant you a kind hand in convincing you, did he?" Pauwel caressed her arms, suddenly aware of his fingers biting into her skin. What was he doing? She'd suffered enough of that sort of thing, he was certain.

"Like you did when you kissed me?" she asked, her brow creased in confusion.

Her uncertainty wounded him. Gods alive, what had Jörg done to her? Had she no concept at all of the respect and care she should have been shown? Apparently not. It was time to teach her. "Like that," he agreed.

She shook her head and buried her face in his chest. He uttered several curses under his breath, and Regana pushed from him as far as his arms would allow.

Pauwel felt his *Blutjagd* spike at that. She was afraid of him, afraid when he was loving and afraid when he was angered. It seemed that no interaction would be safe until Regana learned what was appropriate from a man and what was not. *Damn Jörg!*

"You owe him nothing beyond contempt," he spat. "I cannot even excuse him for his youth and inexperience. He knew. He could not have been tutored by the older women and engaged in all the conversations of the last year and not know.

"I will admit something to you, Regana. He was not the only man who wanted you."

She looked at him in shock.

"Who wants you," he qualified. "Why did I agree to this? Because, I can't live without you." He drew her hand to his erection, still pulsing in his need despite his anger because she was in his arms.

Regana stilled as she realized what he was telling her. Her breathing hitched. She met his eyes, fear warring with confusion in her expression. She didn't know what to expect from him. Considering her past, that wasn't unexpected.

"I want you, Regana. I want ours to be a true marriage, but I will not take you as Jörg took you." Pauwel guided her hand away slowly. "When you are ready to learn tenderness, come to me. Until then, I will ask only what we must present in company."

He kissed her forehead and left the bed. His body screamed at him for what he was doing, and her look of amazement as she surveyed the naked and aroused length of him wasn't helping. Pauwel covered himself quickly, pulling a practice tunic over his head to hide the evidence of his present condition.

"Pauwel?" she called softly.

"Yes?" He kept his voice even, not willing to risk spooking her with a reaction at either extreme that pulled at him.

"I found an amber pendant in your mother's trunk. I tried to give it to Kethe, but she said it wasn't your mother's. She said you had it made for your chosen wife."

Pauwel snapped a look at her. She was more than a little frightened by that concept. What did she need to be at ease? Pauwel would willingly do whatever it was, but he had no idea what Regana sought with that comment. He pulled on his trews, working the lacings as he considered it.

"I had it made for you," he assured her, praying it was the response she'd hoped for.

"Are you sorry...now that you did?" she asked, tears in her eyes.

His eyes widened in shock. "No, I'm not. Someday, you'll wear it for me."

She nodded shakily as he turned away again.

Pauwel kept his back to her as he used the trunk to wrap the bindings for his boots around his legs and fastened his weapons belt around his waist. "I must go. Wedding night or not, I must go to training now."

"I understand," she managed. "I will accompany you tomorrow."

"I would appreciate that," he answered in that same even tone.

"Don't. It is a small boon you ask, much less than I am asking of you."

He faced her in disbelief. "I wouldn't just appreciate it," Pauwel assured her. "I would enjoy it. It's a selfish thing I'm asking."

"Not so selfish. I don't think you're capable of being truly selfish."

"You pay me far more honor than I am due." He left the chamber quickly before he could prove that point. Gods, but his blood was screaming at him to release his morals and take her in the way she was obviously accustomed to. Pauwel couldn't do it, and he knew he would rather face Gawen's blade than give in to it, so he had to leave.

"Will you eat, Pauwel?" Kethe offered as he passed through the main room.

"No. I am late." And he felt as if his appetite would never return, as if Veriel had struck him a gut shot...or one to his sac. In a manner of speaking, that was precisely what had happened, and he was at a loss to undo the damage done.

"Happily so, I am sure."

"Yes," he agreed as he headed for the door, knowing his face would tell his sister more than he wanted her to know.

"Pauwel?"

He paused with his back to her.

"Midday meal," she reminded him as she pressed the food wrapped in a scrap of cloth into his hand.

He nodded and started for the door again, certain that his appetite would not return that soon. "Kethe, see that Regana gets some rest today. This has been a storm of emotion and events for her. She needs to get her bearings."

"I will. Don't concern yourself, Pauwel. I've seen the kind looks she has for you. Regana may be frightened or upset at the turn of events, but she'll soon be the same woman you came to love. Trust me."

Pauwel nodded and headed down the dirt track, through the village, and to the training area.

He snorted at Kethe's parting statements. What he wouldn't give to be able to start over. The best he could hope for was that Regana would come to him and let him teach her the gentler way, to start them off right from here. Pauwel just prayed she'd do that before he lost his mind.